# STARS AND SHADOWS
## BOOK 1

# SUGAR AND SPICE

# KATE RESSMAN

GOLDEN FLEECE PRESS

Golden Fleece Press
PO Box 1464,
Centreville, VA 20122
www.goldenfleecepress.com

Special discounts are available on quantity purchases by corporations, associations, and others. For details, contact the publisher at the address above.
U.S. trade bookstores and wholesalers please contact Ingram Content Group at customerservice@ingramcontent.com or by telephone at 800.973.8000(option 3).

Epub ISBN 13:    978-1-942195-19-1
Mobi ISBN 13:    978-1-942195-20-7
Print ISBN 13:   978-1-942195-16-0
Pdf ISBN 13:     978-1-942195-21-4


Printed in the United States of America

First Edition

10 9 8 7 6 5 4 3 2 1

# DEDICATION

To my parents who have always supported my dreams, my businesses, and started me on the path of reading when I was just a tiny thing.

# ACKNOWLEDGMENTS

This book wouldn't be here if not for the hard work of Julia Ehrmantraut. She not only fought through the initial draft, she discussed world building and addressed the gaping plot holes and the resolution that was missing. She dealt with the not!steampunk cozy that ended up a noir and battered it into submission. Not to mention forcing me to meet deadlines.

I also need to thank my parents for putting up with my writer's retreat. And I cannot forget Kim Roper who came to make sure I saw a human being and ate real food while I was immersed in this universe.

I must also thank Chuck Wendig and his weekly challenges or I wouldn't have written the first story.

# CHAPTER 1

The smog-storm swirled around and over the Long Estate, blinding the outside cameras. The forty-five level structure hung nearly motionless in the buffeting winds of brown and black smoke. The clouds of grit and dust hid the glittering shine of the windows and the ornamentation on the main entrance. Even the red warning lights on the corners that marked out the top, bottom and farthest edges of the Estate were swallowed up. No compounds moved during smog-storms. Even commerce trailers stopped in the middle of the skyways.

Inside the Estate, no hint of the raging winds disrupted the glittering party in the main ballroom. The automatic curtains enveloped the large windows with dazzling displays of light and art. Smaller shields within the rest of the windows extended automatically between the layers of damage-proof glass. Except for one window on the first level of the Pits.

"Piece of smog-borne, devil-swirled excrement," Blagger muttered. He pried open the frame of the window. It banged into his knee. "Mother of a talentless whore!" He was an average sized man with narrow shoulders and hips that allowed him to crawl through access panels and air vents easily. His hair was a mottled brown with dyed streaks of black that made it look like a smog-storm.

"Marsden, sing out, I'm doing paperwork," Gov, the head of Security stated.

"Paperwork" simply indicated something that was being done on the quiet for the lady or something private. Given that it was Gov, who's imagination in private affairs left a lot to be desired, in Blagger's opinion, it was probably just a personnel review.

"You drug-addled, spineless, sex-ravaged hag," Blagger growled at the recalcitrant panel.

"Turn down your radio, Blagger." Marsden's sharp voice cut across the din of chatter on the radios. Marsden, the butler, controlled the entire staff over the radios. Marsden's radio automatically tuned to any of the department head voices and he could contact them directly without the usual "sing out" tag.

"You've heard worse." Marsden didn't respond to the comment. Blagger rubbed his leg, coming away with blood on his fingers. He wiped the blood off on his sturdy green pants. He obediently turned down his radio, cutting off the estate chatter as well as his own transmissions. His ears rang slightly from the lack of noise. This part of the ship was well away from the general public rooms and their ambient chatter. He narrowed his brown eyes at the wiring. He killed the main power to the motor, then pulled it out slowly until he could see the damaged connector. "Gotcha, you little sniggler." He pulled a new part out of his tool pouch and switched them out. The old connector went into the garbage pile for recycling. He turned the power on and watched with a pleased smirk as the shield silently unfolded.

Once everything was cleaned up, he limped down to the Pit Crew's common room. A bit of chilling and a dab of healing cream fixed up his knee. It didn't fix the tear in his pants. He picked at the strands at the edge of the tear, frowning. He shrugged philosophically. He could patch them later. It couldn't make them look any worse. He set out a cold lunch platter for the crew.

Not five minutes after he set out the last piece of cheese a group of twenty dirty, sweaty, happily chattering crew members descended on the room. Blagger grabbed his own plate and set aside three more for the people in the middle of projects. He sprawled on his favorite perch next to the pile of mending projects to exchange jokes and complaints with Tread and Warder—the welders.

"Here, take a look at these for me, would you?" Warder shoved his goggles at him. Blagger shoved a bit of cheese into his mouth. He poked at the button which should have brought down the spark screen to protect the wearer's eyes from the power of the welding light.

"What did you do to them? Shove them into your pouch without the case?"

"Well, maybe." Warder's eyes wandered around the room. The left one drifted a bit slower than the right. The fake eye was blue while his other was the natural brown. It wasn't the only way to tell him apart from his brother, but it took awhile to get used to looking for scars instead of color.

"Get Nurse to look at your eye before you go back out. It's drifting like a top-sail junk boat."

Warder nodded, his black hair falling forward into his face. "Will do. Can you fix them?"

"Yeah. I'll get them done after lunch. How's the rudder looking?"

Tread tapped his glass against his lips. "Well, before the storm, it was shiny and glimmering with bronze and copper detailing." That was a change from the red and blue paint stripes it supposedly had yesterday.

Blagger snorted. "And after?"

"Like the inside of the garbage shoot I'll guess. Job security right?"

Blagger grinned. "So it's moving again? All in one piece?"

"When we left it. Wayland only knows if it's going to still be moving in an hour. Tell Supplies we need a new one."

"I'll put it on the list. Maybe Mel can fabricate one. I think there's enough scrap in the heap."

"Better than nothing. We need to pull it off completely and bring it into the shop," Warder said.

"Next week when the Lady's out."

The two nodded in unison. Blasted twins. Creepy as Ghost-gulls when they got it into their head. "So, what's the word on the party?" Tread asked.

"All the Sugars should be out of the place by Friday. Maintenance sweeps start at midnight. Bottom up. And leftovers in the ballroom are first come-first serve. I take bribes of chocolate and spice currant bread for prime levels."

"Spinner's always said that pork sausage and beer work."

"Last time I looked, you boys weren't Spinner."

They laughed. The Crew finished their meal and dumped the dishes into the washer. The silence left Blagger's ears ringing. He leaned back and folded his hands over his belt. His eyes drifted closed.

----------

Spinner clung to the hull of the Estate as another spiral of storm-wind drove the grit and smog into what little skin her goggles and mask left exposed on her face. The small sensors she'd just fixed retreated into their protective covering. She patted the cover with a smile. It was always encouraging to see your work in action.

"Sensor alarm 11 resolved," Penny informed her. "Helion sensor alarm still chiming. No response from unit."

"No response?" Digg asked. "Probably because he's not there." Spinner laughed into the muffling canvas over her face like the rest of the crew. The Helion was Branch's responsibility and that bastard was never where he should be. She contemplated embroidering the edges of the mask again as she maneuvered toward the doors.

"Anyone told Blagger his radio's still off?" she asked.

The rest of the Pit Crew muttered negatives. They didn't want to spoil her fun. She smirked as she heard them scatter back to tasks while she was shedding the extra layers of the exterior work harness. There were two layers of the hull. The crew had taken over the inner layer for storing the equipment which was only used outside. The work-harnesses were hung in neat rows—battered leather and canvas, stained with lubricant, sweat, and smog-grit.

She shoved the heavy outside gloves into the box. It was the last pair that would fit now that everyone was inside. It was surprisingly quiet between the hulls. The howl of the wind and the drone of the motor somehow didn't reach into this pocket of space. Or maybe she was just going deaf.

She shoved the screwdriver that was hanging off of her belt into her work-pouch. The red embroidery was starting to fray. She'd fix it before bed. She'd better check Blagger's. He'd never mention it—just try to fix it himself and destroy the whole thing.

She stomped off some of the grit and grime—not that anyone would notice in the Pit. Every surface except for the top of the food tables was covered in a fine mess of dust, smog-grit, grease, and flakes of metal. She'd only seen Nurse twice before breaking herself of the habit of rubbing her eyes.

Tread waved cheerfully as he headed toward the scrap room. She drew up the fabrication list in her mind. Probably the dart panel for the runabout shuttle. It would take at least a day and the storm meant they couldn't work on the secondary dock doors. There was a muted wave of noise as she passed the main quarters. The daily shift deals were being hammered out. Spinner shook her head. No one ever tried to make deals with her.

Blagger was leaning back almost asleep. At least to the

casual observer. He was waiting to make sure everyone ate and to store away the meager leftovers. Time to make him jump.

----------

The door clanged open. Spinner clomped into the room, peeling off her smog-mask. She let it hang around her neck. She pushed her goggles up to the top of her head over her tousled dirty blonde hair. The heat had exacerbated the normal curl, leaving her with a head of ringlets.

"Someone spiked the Helion Circuit."

Blagger blinked. The Helion Circuit was the main control circuit for the steering mechanism. Granted they didn't move the Estate often, but losing the circuit made them a sitting target for Cities. "What idiot'd do that? Especially in a storm like this?" If he didn't take the bait, he'd never know the end of the joke.

"No idea, but if we don't fix it, it's a sure thing that the Sugar-Nobs will blame one of us."

"Leave it to Branch. The Lady will understand the delay. I'm not taking responsibility for that man's sex life. Eat some lunch." He waved a hand toward the stored plates.

She took one of the plates and sat down at the iron table. She peeled off her gloves, then folded her hands. She'd been working on the scrubbers and you could see the outline of her goggles on her face. Her hands were a good three shades lighter than the rest of her skin. She bowed her head. He'd never asked her who she prayed to and she'd repaid the favor. There were too many gods in the world to risk the argument that might come out of it. It was something he'd learned early in the London. He guessed she'd picked the habit up in Amsterdam. The Estate-born folks didn't always understand that he didn't want to talk about religion or politics, but Spinner, she always understood keeping quiet.

"How did you hear about the circuit anyway?" The

storm was too loud to over-hear conversations and
nothing had come over the radio. She blinked at him, then
reached up to take out her earplugs. Blagger scratched
behind his ear. He smacked into his radio. He jumped as
sound flooded his ears.

Spinner laughed. "If you don't turn your radio on, you
miss all the good gossip. Alarm's chiming and Branch isn't
answering it."

Blagger rolled his eyes at that. He pulled the radio off
and rubbed his ear. He turned down the volume and
cautiously placed it back over his ear. He gestured rudely at
her. She crossed her eyes at him and mimed an even
cruder symbol. He brightened and raised his brows. She
glared at him. He shrugged. It had been worth the try. "So
who do you like for it? One of the new techs?"

Spinner was quiet for a moment. Her grey eyes shifted
out of focus. "No, they don't go to the wheelhouse.
Branch wouldn't break anything he can't fix. The Crusts
are too busy working because of the party. Even the
visiting ones. No, it's one of the Sugars."

"They wouldn't know how to find it or know how to
break it."

"Unless they weren't born a Sugar. Or they aren't one
really right now. Think about it, if you or I were to say,
clean up and swirl around that party, no one would notice
that we're not Sugars. I'm sure a Sugar could do the same
thing under the floors."

Blagger frowned. The Helion was set to only alarm
when it was completely non-functional. Otherwise they'd
have alarms every time the Estate moved in a storm.
Branch was certified on it, but every member of the Pits
was trained on taking it out or putting it in. Too bad they
didn't have a spare; he'd just have Mica switch it out. Blast.
"We'll talk more after you finish eating. Smog'll blow you
right away." Spinner had a bad habit of skipping her meals.
She rolled her eyes at him, but started eating again. There
were still two Crew members who hadn't come in for a

break. "Tungsten, Branch, you coming in for lunch?"

"I give it ten minutes," Tungsten said. "Just need to finish reconnecting these wires."

"Branch? Sing out." The chatter reduced at the command. There was no sound from Branch. "Mel, can you check on Branch? Make sure he's got his radio on?" Branch was a regular lay-about. When he wasn't sleeping on the job, he was enjoying the attentions of one of the crust women. His wife, Mel's mother, had died when she was just a tot. It seemed Branch was constantly auditioning replacements. Mel herself was used to walking in on his tryouts.

"Sure thing." Mel's voice was cheerful and bright like a child's toy. The crew stayed dead quiet and the rest of the estate seemed to be similarly quiet. "He's not in the wheel room. He was working on the casing today, right?"

"Yes. Marsden, we need a searcher."

"I'm sending Wolston to do a look."

Mel's voice came back, bleak, "Don't bother. I found him."

"Gov, get down to the wheel-room," Marsden ordered. "Nurse, to the wheel-room."

"I'll tell Gov," Security's second-in-command stated. "He's still off radio."

"I'm coming, Mel," Blagger told her. "Spin?"

Spinner nodded. She shoved another piece of cheese into her mouth and tucked away a piece of bread in her pocket to eat on the way. They made their way down the back passage to the emergency pole. It was the fastest way down to the bottom level. Blagger clicked his safety harness into place. He glared until Spinner did the same. She rolled her eyes at him and shoved the bread into her mouth before stepping out and sliding down the pole with one arm and one leg wrapped around it.

"Show-off." Blagger wrapped both arms and legs around the pole and followed her. The wind of the journey screamed past him. He dropped down into the padded cushion and promptly fell over backward. Spinner offered him a hand with a sweet smile. He accepted it. He'd had all his pride kicked out of him years ago.

They found Mel in the wheel room, tears streaming down her face. Blagger held out his arms and she curled up on his shoulder. He ran his hand over her short-cropped, kinky hair. She wore it shorter than her father did. Blagger closed his eyes for a moment, then looked over to where Spinner was crouched down next to Branch. His hair was spread like a halo around his head. The gritty salt and pepper coloring of it was thankfully not marred with blood. His eyes were open a shade too wide.

Gov showed up with Nurse and two security investigators. The investigators, Blaisedale and Metro, he thought they were called, started recording the entire area. They would have to secure the area with hopes that the storm would burn itself out quickly enough to call the Nobs. If not, they'd have to preserve the body for an official death declaration. Nurse, a sturdy woman with a pristine white pantsuit, took the pulse that wasn't there. No one expected there to be one. He was too limp. And then there was the acrid smell that bled under the normal smells of oil and dust.

Mel sniffled into Blagger's chest. He gave her a rough cotton handkerchief with swirls of purple on it. She gave him a weak smile and blew her nose. She didn't give it back as she continued to sniffle. She refused to look at her father's body. Spinner had no such trouble. She was examining the man from every angle she could without touching him. Her fingers rested lightly on the ground as she got a good look at his skin. The implants in her eyes flickered as she narrowed her sight. Who knew what she was seeing in the spectrums above and below baseline.

----------

Mel was leaking into Blagger's handkerchief. Spinner averted her eyes quickly to give the young woman some privacy to grieve her father. Branch's neck was broken and there wasn't any bruising near his windpipe. His eyes had the glassy, fixed look of a dead fish. Spinner narrowed her eyes and activated her implants. The official records said that her implants registered the enhanced spectrum, but the mother of the temple had arranged for a few extras that the Authorities never recorded. Branch was cold. He'd been dead for at least four hours—the beginning of shift. If it hadn't been for the storm someone might have noticed.

She tuned out the radio chatter and focused on the measurements. She glanced up at the hollow behind his head and noted the purposefully scuffed footprints. She let her eyes drift across the feet of the others in the room before calculating the angle of the force which had broken his neck and the height of the killer.

Metro crouched down to record the scene. He smelled of mint and comfrey. "Stomach bothering you again?" Spinner asked.

He snorted. "It wasn't." He chose a few long angles—adding measurements with his pen. "What have you touched?"

"My prints are on file." She focused on the doors. There had to be traces that were missed by the killer. Spinner shifted her eyes to the floorboards. Metro frowned at her, but didn't stop her investigation.

----------

"Marsden, what's the weather look like?" Blagger called.

The butler sighed. "It's smog for at least the next two days. We've got a scheduled City coming through day after that. Branch?"

"Dead."

Marsden stifled his curse until it came out more like a growl. "Mel?"

"I've got her. We'll send her with Nurse tonight."

"What does that do to your schedules?"

"We'll take care of it. Could do with someone to take care of lunch and breakfast though? Some platters made up, something like that."

"Cookie?"

"I'm on it, Dearie," Cookie answered immediately. " I'll send one of the boys down with some cold platters and some whiskey for the wake."

"Thanks, Cookie." Blagger tightened his hold on Mel. "We'll need a day."

"Understood. Emergencies only. Of course, you know that means the toilets will stop working." Marsden's voice was dry and Blagger had to smirk. "Keep me informed. Gov, I've contacted the Authorities. They say to secure the body. Keep it cold. Lock everyone out of the area."

"Funny that, Marsden," Blagger stated. "He's in the Wheel Room. We can't lock everyone out. Emergency protocol in case the tether fails.

"Who's the pilot scheduled to move us? No one else in or out."

"That'll be Perky or me. And we'll need the Helion functional in case we need to actually need to move," Blagger said. Branch and Perky were the normal pilots, but Blagger wasn't about to let Perky walk into an uncleaned wheelroom.

The chatter across the lines picked up as an issue swept down from the ballroom. Blagger tuned out of the chatter and focused on Spinner. She was checking the doors for something. Metro was following her with the camera while Blaisdale started the more formal process of verbal and written documentation of the scene. Mel would need to be interviewed. And Blagger would have to lay out the schedules. He pulled out his datapad and stared sending over the documentation that would be needed. He didn't like any of his people for it, but that didn't mean they hadn't seen or heard something.

"Hey! Stop that," Metro snapped as Spinner scraped something off of the doorframe into an isolation jar. She looked down her nose at him.

"Relax. I'm going to give it to you and it's on camera."

"Oh, right." Metro was new to the Estate. He'd been a Nob on the Krakow, but came to the Estate as an investigator with his fiancée, Duchess. Duchess worked in the kitchens, but they still weren't married. It had been nearly three years now. Blagger's money was on the breakup happening within the next two months. Marsden was holding the action on it. Two months had fourteen to one odds. It'd get him a good case of vodka out of the kitchens if he won. Metro was a tall, willowy man, with a sharp enough mind when he chose to use it. His eyes were a bright, augmented green. He could take measurements in an instant. He wore a discrete gold hoop in each ear that made Marsden twitch every time he saw them. Blagger approved.

Blaisdale on the other hand had been born on the Estate and would probably die there. He was a portly man with brown hair that was starting to turn grey. His eyes were brown and the only augmentation he had was a replacement finger. He'd lost his index finger on an ill-advised attempt to work with heavy equipment. His father had been the best welder on the estate. The Pit Crew considered him one of their own. Smart, Blagger thought. There'd be no question of whether the crew would be honest with him. "Blagger, who knows how to pull the Circuit?"

Blagger snorted. "The whole crew. Everyone's trained on it, in case of emergencies. Maybe three or four of the Kitchen. The Lady. Marsden. And I've got a handful of others, I'm sure. I'll work on the list."

Blaisdale grunted. "Of course." He gave Mel's shoulder a squeeze. "Come talk to me, Mel. Then, we'll send you off with Nurse."

She nodded. She took off her radio and tucked it into her pouch. "Of course, Blaise."

"You call me when you get to bed," Blagger ordered gently.

She gave him a quick hug. Blagger joined Spinner at the

control panel. "Let me take a look."

Spinner bumped him with her shoulder. "See what there is to see first."

"Like the fact that there's no damage to the panel?"

"Exactly."

"How long to pull it?" Metro asked.

"Without damage, by someone who knows what they're doing?" Blagger considered. "It'd take me about fifteen minutes. I need to see what's behind the panel though to see if they did it right or just threw some lipstick on the front to hide it."

Spinner cocked her head to the side. "It'd take me about twenty minutes. I think the fastest person would be Wen. Hey, Wen, sing out, how long to pull the Helion?"

"Twelve minutes," Wen's gravelly voice told them. "Perfect conditions and I knew I needed to do it."

Metro nodded and made a note. "Twelve minutes minimum. More than likely half an hour for someone who doesn't know exactly how ours is set up?"

"Standard build on this section. We make sure it stays that way so anyone can use the emergency directions." Blagger tapped the top of the console. "Blaise, Metro, I'm opening the panel to see what sort of damage is under there. Marsden, who reported the circuit missing?"

"Got a malfunction alarm in my office that it was off-line. But we've got alarms all over the place from the storm." Marsden sounded distracted. Blagger went down on one knee and removed the access panel. "But who told you it had been snagged?"

"Digg?"

"I heard it from, let's see, Patsy."

"Patsy, sing out."

"I didn't report anything. I've been in the transporter 3. It's still giving us fits on the first Kitchen level."

"Come to the common room," Blaisedale broke in. "I'll talk to you there."

"Right, Blaise."

The wires were a mess, but they weren't broken. It was the loss of the unit they usually rested on that made them hang in random patterns. He traced the wires with his eyes. "It was someone who knows what they're doing," he confirmed. "There's no damage to the control units. And we've still got running lights. We can start up the engines and move in whichever direction we went in last."

"Give me a worst case flight plan and I'll contact the other Estates and London."

"Will do."

Spinner rested a hand on his shoulder as she peered into the unit. "There are prints. Metro, aim the camera in there with filter U on."

Blagger moved out of the way. "Got it," Metro said.

Spinner toyed with a curl. "Nobs are going to blame this on the Pit."

"You're paranoid," Metro said. He put the camera down. "There are good police detectives."

"Not coming to this estate. Last three sets were fixed on looking only under the floors."

Blaisdale snorted. "Don't try to change the Princess' mind, Metro. She hates Nobs."

Spinner rolled her eyes. "They keep proving me right by sending idiots."

Marsden cut across the chatter again, "London is pinging us about a tether malfunction. They want us to move moorings. I'm pushing them off, citing the storm. They say they've got some drift too and to be aware. Gov," he called out to the head of security "get people on finding that Circuit. We've got forty-eight hours before they just cut us loose and I do not want to explain that to Mistress Long if I don't have to."

# CHAPTER 2

Gov scowled at Blagger. "What are we looking for exactly? Talk to Velvet and Honey."

"Do I have to?" Blagger shifted his weight from side to side. Spinner bit her lips and looked down. He'd had a fling with both of them. At the same time. Gov had to know that.

"Why do you make life so difficult? Just describe the damned circuit for them." Gov was a former military man with sharp grey eyes and straight shoulders. He kept himself in fighting condition and Blagger wanted to throw down with him someday, just to see who'd win. Gov was trained, but Blagger was mean and he played dirty.

"I'll do it," Spinner offered. She squeezed Blagger's arm. She certainly knew about the flings.

"No, that's okay. I'll meet them in the common room. With reinforcements," he muttered, glancing at her. Spinner looked around the room, her eyes flickering through the spectrum. He wondered what the world looked like to her sometimes. He was the only person on the Crew who didn't have some sort of augmentation yet. He wasn't sure what that said about him.

"Don't look at me to protect you," Spinner stated. "I'm

just going to get a cup of coffee and watch them beat you."

Gov paused and looked over at them. "For frilly's sake. Tell me you didn't."

"Well," Blagger shrugged.

Gov looked impressed. "I didn't think Velvet went for men."

"It was a good year to wear him down." Blagger rubbed his fingernails on his vest. The dirt under the tips ruined the move.

Gov huffed. "Keep it in your damned pants. If you piss them off, I won't investigate the murder."

Blagger gave the head of security a flourished bow. Then, he started for the transporter back up to the common room. He paused at the door. He opened the control panel. "I'm locking out everyone except Security and the Lady. Anyone else needs to get in, they have to come with one of them." Gov nodded approval.

Spinner held the door to the transporter open. "Wait a minute," she glanced at the walls. "Metro, we need a camera in here to record prints."

"I want your implants," Metro said. "Measurements are great, don't get me wrong, but the spectrum seems so much more useful."

"Check your specs. I think there's more in the package that you're not using yet."

Metro raised his brows. "I will. I've had them for years though." He shot the inside of the transporter. "I thought three was out of service."

"It is. This is six."

"No, the schematics say this is three." Metro frowned and stared at the wall. "Are you sure?" It was obvious that he was trying to recall the blueprints that hung on the back walls in the main serving corridor. The main service corridor ran behind the public spaces of the estate to let the Crusts run the estate without being seen.

"That's the original sheet. You need the as-built copies." This is six." Blagger said. He transferred a copy to

Metro's pad. "I've sent you a copy."

"Is it traditionally three here?"

"This is a mirror-build estate." Blagger pointed across the room. "At the Mimsy Estate, that side is Transporters seven through twelve and this side is one through six. Imagine someone took the original blueprints and flipped them upside down and then worked from them. We're flipped front to back too," he explained. "Wheel house is on the opposite side. I'll have Mel sit down with you and walk you through the differences." Metro had only been below the floors a handful of times. The upper levels all looked the same, mirror build or not. He nodded his thanks and let them leave.

----------

The door slid shut and the elevator was silent. Spinner tucked her radio away. Blagger raised a brow, but followed suit. It was one thing she loved about him—he trusted her. "Branch wasn't killed by the thief." She stopped the elevator.

She waited as Blagger's eyes darted up toward the security camera. "What do you mean?" he asked. It was shaded with tones of "*is this my problem?*" and "*Stars, do I know the killer?*"

"The thief didn't want to be noticed. Whoever killed Branch did it from behind. They snuck up behind him and broke his neck. If it were the thief, they would have had to be coming back for something else. This was Estate business." She glanced down at her wrist to indicate timing. Branch was notorious for turning off his radio and sneaking away for a tryst. The engine room was his favorite hiding spot.

"Tell that to Gov."

"He won't listen." Why should he? He'd snapped Branch's neck neatly enough. Now, if she could just prove it from more than just her gut. She could have done it, but there weren't many people with her training running around the Long estate. At least, she didn't know them yet.

"He doesn't like me playing in his sandbox without changing departments."

"Yeah. I understand the impulse." Blagger crossed his arms over his chest. Spinner reached up and pinched his cheeks.

"You're so cute when you get possessive."

"I know what you're going to do."

"I should hope so. Red dress or yellow, do you think?" It would be yellow, of course, his favorite color.

"Gov's going to pitch a fit."

She rolled her eyes. "We need the Helion before London cuts our mooring and we slam into them."

"Velvet and Honey are more than capable."

Of finding the thief? No doubt. Fingering the killer, no. Spinner needed to talk to Lady Long. "Of blending with Sugars? Sure. Of stopping fights? Yes. Of finding blackmailers? No doubt. Finding a circuit that can be hidden inside something? No."

Blagger studied her for a long moment. "I'm not going to ask questions I don't want answered. We can't talk to them about Branch."

"Military man. Your height. Knows this Estate better than his own hand. With motive." Gov's fiancée had been stepping out with Branch for two months. Blagger told her that the day it started. He'd heard the radio chatter.

He took a breath and held it. He released it in a rush.

"Fine. I'll find something suitable on my bunk, I'm sure."

"Indeed." She winked, then put her radio back on. Blagger followed suit.

----------

"Sing out, Blagger."

"What's up, Marsden?"

"Don't go off-line without warning." The butler paused. "I have been reliably informed that you're alone in a transporter with Spinner. Do not stay on-line without warning for that either."

"Yes, sir." Blagger tipped an imaginary hat to the camera that was in the transporter. "I'll ask you to let me wipe that footage."

"In your tiny, little dreams, Blagger," Honey informed him.

"You wound me, sweetheart, you do."

"Honey," Gov snapped.

"Right. No flirting until we have the information. After that though, I'm calling fair game."

"I'm expecting someone in that room to think with the right head," the head of security growled.

Marsden snorted. Spinner's laughter bent her in two. Velvet purred, "But, Gov, it is the right head when it comes to Blagger. It's the easiest way to communicate."

"Jesus. Stop it. I do not want to know."

Blagger could just imagine Gov's hand held out in front with the other over his eyes. It was the same posture he pulled out whenever he walked in on something he didn't want to have to know about. Like that one time with the socialator and the Lord in flagrante in the Lady's sitting room. What a messy one that had been. Honey sent Spinner off with a pat to the ass that made Blagger think twice. He exchanged a look with Velvet. "You have to admit, it'd be fun to watch."

"You are disgusting, Blagger."

"And you love it."

Velvet was light skinned, with soft black hair that curled intriguingly around his ears and an almost permanent shadow on his cheeks. His eyes were vermillion due to implants that let him see heat signatures. His cupid bow lips and fine features made the rumors about him being a wrong-sheeted Sugar on the Lady's side more probable. His voice was soft and soothing. He was starting to develop smile lines around his eyes. He also did this thing with his tongue when he was kissing that Blagger desperately wanted to learn.

Honey was two inches taller than he was, with a

striking head full of braids. Her skin had the rose-brown tone of the wildflower honey that she was named for. Her eyes were non-augmented brown. She wore three inch heels on a regular basis and her dress clung in all the right places. It showed off her chest and her hips to great effect. She wore a stunning amount of eye make-up today, obviously coming off of party duty to talk to him.

"What are we looking for?" she asked. She tugged on a loose piece of Blagger's hair.

"It's about sixteen centimeters square. The outside is coated with a noxiously green color that can't be missed."

"Sixteen centimeters square. In thirty floors of rooms." Velvet groaned. "Gov, can we grab more people?"

"No. This has to be done on the sly or we'll have a panic on our hands, and there's nowhere for that to go."

Honey bit her lip. She turned down her radio and started to curse. About three minutes later, she wound down. Velvet looked at her with stars in his eyes. Blagger rubbed his ears. "Sweet mother of stars, woman. That was painful." She turned her radio back on.

"Really, people, no going off-line without telling me," Marsden snapped.

"Didn't mean to worry you, Boss." Honey winced. "I didn't want to clutter the line with useless information."

"I don't want anyone alone until the killer is located. This means all of you. Heads, come up with duty rosters and send them to the front office."

"Yes, sir," echoed from all the units.

"Nurse, you have Mel tonight, yes?"

"Yes, Blagger."

"Pit Crew, we've got the day tomorrow. I want everyone in the common room. If you have to leave the room, you take someone with you. I don't care if it's just to take a leak. Hear?"

"Heard," replied the multiple voices that were his crew.

"Great, now I just need to get a leash on Spinner and we're good."

"Sounds like fun. Why weren't you that adventurous when we were together?" Honey ran a finger down his nose.

"I was. You weren't interested. Lack of imagination."

Velvet laughed at that. "Come on, Honey. Let's tackle the improbable. The impossible will have to wait until after dinner." He offered his arm and the two of them left the Pit as quickly as possible. Blagger turned into the crew quarters and found his way to the room he shared with Spinner. They had two small beds with comfortable mattresses, shoved together in the center of the room. A pile of rugs and blankets filled the corner for when the temperatures started to fluctuate during flight. Laying across the bed was the suit Spinner expected him to wear. He hadn't touched it in at least a year, but the fabric was still good. He could get away without the jacket this late in the party, but he might want it to hide his knife.

He hung up his tool pouch and goggles on their hook. He tucked his fingerless gloves into the pouch. He left his clothes in a heap under his tools. It wasn't as though he was going to clean them this early in the week. The built in fibers helped them shed odors and oil and dirt, but didn't make them particularly comfortable. Not like the silk of the shirt and the cotton of the suit he'd be wearing shortly. He stepped into the sanitizer.

Spinner looked over her shoulder at him. "Get my back." He scrubbed her back, doing his best to get the smog and grit off of her skin. She did the same for him. He washed her hair while she worked on her face and arms. The delicate swirls of her tattoos finally started to show, just a shade darker than her skin. They spread across her shoulders and over her chest like an ornate piece of lacework. Blagger's own tattoos were less delicate and stood out boldly against his paler skin.

A fine fretwork of scars decorated the backs of her hands and up her arms. He rinsed her hair out once more until it gleamed in the harsh light of the room. He scrubbed his own head for a few minutes, until the rinse came away clear. Squeaky clean, they stepped back into the main room and got dressed. Spinner turned to let him zip up the sleeveless yellow dress. It showed off her tattoos, which most would mistake for make-up in the Sugar realm. It was the latest craze, delicate tattoos made of vegetable dyes; aping the Pits and the Crusts who'd been wearing real tattoos for years.

The tattoos on his arms meant something to the people who could read them. The gang he'd worked for as a youth, the master he'd apprenticed under, the many specialties he'd gathered over the years were all written in his skin. Spinner's tattoos were just as telling, but he couldn't read them. They were religious, was all she'd told him. He traced the line across her back with a finger. "Need help with your hair?"

"I think I can manage." She poked him in the arm. "Suit up and I'll make sure you look the part."

"One annoying Sugar trying too hard, coming right up." He winked at her. He pulled on the pants and added a tooled leather belt with a toolkit in the buckle. He strapped his knife to his ankle. Then, he buttoned up the sheer, white silk shirt. His tattoos would show through the fabric. He added a black vest with brown trace-work that let him add a zap-gun to the small of his back. He slipped a datapad into the front pocket and then added an old-fashioned pocket-watch. Another thing that marked him as a front-running Sugar dandy. Young and stupid enough with his money to buy a watch that wouldn't even run. Well, let them assume it didn't. He rubbed the front absently with his thumb. His lover had given it to him before her death. The engraved "H" always evoked a wave of memories.

Spinner added some product to his hair to make it spike up and around in a messy tangle. Her own hair was a shiny, glossy mass of waves that stayed close to her head. She'd done make-up. Her eyes were enhanced by a bit too much black make-up and she had small orange stones in each ear. The rest of the crew might think they were fake, but Blagger knew real gems when he saw them. He raised his brows and leaned closer. "Where'd you find those?"

"Around." She shrugged carelessly. The skirt of her dress fell down below her knee and flared at the hip, trimming her waist and helping to hide the muscles of her thighs. She wore a pair of dancing shoes with a one inch heel and had applied a delicate rose decoration that ran up and around her left leg – declaring that she was dating, but not yet engaged. Blagger kissed her hand, then offered his arm.

Then, he put in his radio. "God damn it, Blagger!"

"Sorry, meant to warn, I was with Spinner in the sanitizer."

"I'm going to have you gelded."

"Right, Boss. We're going to take a walk."

Marsden sighed. "Princess Spinner decided she has to look, didn't she? Can't you do something about that?"

Blagger rolled his eyes at Spinner. "I think you've got a strange idea of the power dynamic in this relationship."

"You're already talking like a Sugar. Fine. Don't annoy the Lady."

"I think we can manage that. We'll be off radio."

"No, you will not."

"We're going to a Party," Spinner said cheerfully, into Blagger's radio.

# CHAPTER 3

Blagger tucked Spinner's hand into the crook of his arm. She accepted the action with well-worn patience. Her shoulders settled back and her chin lifted. The dress shifted just slightly as she moved her legs closer together and she was suddenly a Sugar. He straightened his own shoulders and cocked his head towards her as though he was listening to something she'd just said as the doors opened.

The sound washed over them. It was more than the chatter or clanging they'd hear in the crew common room. There were only about 600 Sugars in attendance. But the band was playing some new dance and the people were attempting to talk over and around the strength of the beat and the soaring, sharp strings. Crystal and silver clinked and clanked around the room. Laughter—genuine and not—spiraled across the top of everything. Spinner and Blagger ignored that and continued what appeared to be a discrete conversation. People would politely pretend not to see them returning from what was obviously the servant's quarters.

Blagger's fingers itched to test out his skills on these glittering fools. There were diamonds and colored gems dangling from wrists and copper and bronze around the high necks and low ankles. Crystal and light diodes from years ago offered a counterpoint to the streams of lights and stars that made up the emergency screen distractions. Bright colors washed over the crowd, making it difficult to decide what colors the women were wearing. The men were almost all in black and white, the better to show off their attachments in small spots of color and tiny digital pictures of wrists and hands that they wore on their chest. Blagger made a note of that. He'd have to acquire one soon enough, or they'd be too behind the times to blend in.

"Just maneuver us through the crowd until we can make it to the transporters. I want to start looking immediately."

"Wait a second, love. Can't you do that thing you usually do and at least give us some likely suspects?"

She rolled her eyes at him and gave him a fake little laugh. "All right, so get us to a good vantage point so that I can find people for you to pull dossiers on." He danced them between the couples, greeting women with a tip of an imaginary hat and the men with a hearty backslap that left them not willing to call him out on being a stranger. There were so many people at a common gathering like this that the possibility of remembering everyone you'd met under the influence of some very nice wine was nearly impossible. He plucked two glasses of five proof from the tray of a passing waiter with a spinning turn. The waiter's impassive face flashed into a swift smile and then away. Willy was a nice guy, always generous with his body and his supply of the wine. Blagger winked at him.

He offered Spinner one of the glasses. She sipped and smiled over the top of it. He returned the smile and stepped into her personal space. Let everyone think they were still in the first throws of attraction. "Brown and red hair with the green tie." Blagger glanced in the direction of her eyes.

"Noted."

They continued on through the crowd. "Blue and yellow tie with black hair."

"Noted." He danced her through the crowd on the ballroom floor. The other couples were as wrapped up in each other as he and Spinner appeared to be. There were a few turned heads, but they were admiring looks, not suspicious.

"Pink stripes."

"Noted." Blagger's eyes met Mistress Long's. She was wearing a floor-length grey dress with a slit that showed off flashes of the lily that she wore on her ankle to show that she was married. Her brown hair had swirls of yellow through it. It was pulled up onto the top of her head with a coil of copper wire arranging it in a cascade. A single drop of diamond dangled off of her throat. Her violet eyes narrowed in on him, then widened. The rest of her face didn't change. She turned her head to the woman she was speaking with. Spinner smirked at him. "What? She knows we've good reason. She's got her radio."

Spinner shook her head. "The rumors about the two of you have always amused me. She has better taste." They moved through the intricate dace until they reached the stage of the band. They rested there, watching the crowd move through the each other in a swirl of dresses and glitter. "Body glitter is offensive," Spinner stated. "There's simply no need for that."

"It comes and it goes. Works well with the distraction lighting, I think. We could scatter some over the sheets," he whispered into her ear. His eyes caught on a familiar face. He couldn't remember where he'd seen the man before. He was older than most of the dancers—possibly Lord Long's age. He kept the frown off his face by force of will. He made note though.

"Who?"

"Old man in the grey."

"Didn't think he was your type."

Interesting. Spinner didn't notice anything. He shrugged. "He's cute enough. And older men are experienced."

"You'd know." She leaned into his side.

"White dress and the chopped off hair. Just out of the service."

"Noted."

"Green suit."

"Noted. And his tailor must be having a fit to have created something that truly ugly." The lapels were too thin and there was a stripe of something shiny running down the flared leg. Blagger hoped that would never catch on. He wouldn't wear it even if it did.

"Trying to stand out."

"He doesn't have the moves to do that. Can't manage a simple figure dance."

"Where is the one in purple and white headed? Can you see? She's a bit too small for me."

"I have her. Heading toward the servant's quarters." He hastily substituted "servant" for Crusts and Crumbs. It was one of the few trips he'd always had trouble with.

"We'll check on her later then."

"I've got the boy in the white suit with the vest in rainbows. Have you seen that watch on his chain? It's original."

"Really? How can you tell?"

"I'll teach you someday. Things you pick up."

"And the one with the dragon tattoo crawling up his neck."

"Marked. Shall we move to the wall near the buffet? It'll be a bit quieter there." They would be behind the speakers for the band.

----------

Spinner shrugged against his arm. Her eyes trailed over the crowd. "Might as well." He offered his arm and led her toward the buffet. They didn't partake, but they did take a good look for the next day. Blagger would be able to request anything left over for the wake. It would be an honor. He stationed them on the stools behind the buffet. They could see clearly and everyone would think they were sharing an intimate drink. "Black hair with the silver earrings."

"Noted." Blagger had an excellent memory for faces. He'd practiced for years.

"Do you know any of them?"

"By reputation. Not in an more interesting way."

"You mean you haven't worked your way with that girl in the pink confection of a dress? She seems like one of yours."

Blagger turned to look across the room. Spinner could tell exactly when he saw her. A mischievous smile crossed his face. "Little Miss? Oh she was the lady's too. She's a socialator. Worked in London proper for a few years. I assume she's here with someone." He cocked his head to the side. "Or else the Master of the House has made some arrangements for the unattached gentlemen."

Spinner sipped her five percent and nibbled at a small piece of dark chocolate. It was a treat they never got below decks. She missed it. "Think you can get her to talk to you?"

"I'm sure of it." He absently kissed her temple. She allowed it as part of the cover. Normally, he gave her more warning before things like that. He looked across the room and met the woman's eyes.

She was a petite, round woman with long, straight brown hair that she wore coiled up on top of her head in a messy knot. Tendrils dangled behind her ears, drawing attention to her throat. She had sparkling lengths dangling off of it. They changed color as she moved her head. Around her neck was a chain of gold that wrapped around her throat three times. Her dress was a light confection of ruffles and pink ribbons. It was twenty years out of date. She looked better than half the younger women and better than all the rest of the older women.

She winked at Blagger. She drifted through the crowd. She accepted a few discrete dangles. A young man slid a hand up her hip to touch her ribs. She batted his hand away with a sharp word and the dandy retreated. His cheeks were red. He held his hand to his chest as the other men laughed. He had to learn at some point how to properly approach a high-quality socialator. Soon, or he'd be in bigger trouble. She ended up next to the buffet. Her skirts settled around her with an artificial swirl.

She studied the displayed sweets. She chose a one-bite strawberry jam crumble square.

"Miss," Blagger greeted with a gentle inclination of his head. Spinner hid a smile. That was the sort of movement that could only be learned through use. Practice was not enough. Little Miss smiled sweetly.

"James," she named him. "It's so nice to see you again." She stepped around the table and approached the two of them. "And I see someone has finally captured your attention."

"Spinner, this is Miss. She's from London."

Spinner offered a discrete hand. They shook in the shadow of Little Miss' body. "You look lovely, Spinner." She looked a little more closely. "Your artwork is spectacular. I haven't seen anything that delicate in years. Have you been taking good care of this scamp?" She angled her body toward the two of them flirtatiously.

"I do my best. He's a handful."

"She's such a peach." Little Miss laughed and leaned closer. "What's the what?"

"Looking for a thief who isn't one of us. Specializing in circuitry. Or anyone with military service."

"You have a datapad? I can send you a list. If you've very nice to me, I might even be able to send it to you before the end of the night."

"Oh, lovely, just say the word."

She smacked him gently on the shoulder with a finger. "Be good. Spinner doesn't appreciate that sort of behavior,

I'm sure."

"It's Blagger. How can I not?" Spinner smiled. "I would love to take you back to my room and share stories, but it's a bit too small for comfort."

"Don't worry. Mine isn't. Room 1548. James knows the knock."

"Any time I should avoid?"

"Oh, no, they're still playing for the privilege."

----------

"Still owning the world I see. Good," Blagger said. She'd taught him so much over the six months she'd trained him.

"A little practice here and there. I'll talk to Monet as well. She's my companion on this trip."

"Are you traveling with the Sugars then or on your own?" Blagger raised his brows.

"I'm following the Season. I'm an independent. I do so love the parties here though. The company is so much more interesting. And Lady Long isn't interested in all the games."

"Configure your comm unit to frequency 78 and you'll reach me directly," Spinner told her. "Let us know if there's anything you see that's out of the ordinary."

"Oh, darling girl, it's all ordinary now. A bunch of posturing children. No matter how old they get." She blew a kiss to each of them and moved off.

"Is she traveling with a servant?" Spinner frowned.

"We can check. I'm going to assume that she's not. She's never liked the idea of having to share her space with anyone. And she's got a lovely little speedster that doesn't take kindly to too many people."

Velvet approached them from a careful angle. He stopped a few feet away. He chose a single bite of sweetcake. He bit into it. "Anything I need to know?"

"Don't bother with Little Miss." Blagger approached the table from behind. "Not her business."

Velvet nodded. "She's lovely."

"She's beyond your means."

"Ah well. A man can still dream."

"And he can see if she's interested in a non-business arrangement. Such things do happen. I think you'd make a lovely picture," Spinner told him.

"I think Honey might have words for me. And they would not be words I enjoyed. Have you found anything useful?"

"We'll have a list of suspects in about an hour or so. I'll pass them on via your pad."

Spinner spent the time sizing up the rest of the room. "I think you and Honey need to get over to the band area. There's something brewing between two of the dandies. There's a woman between them right now, but she's about to throw one of them over for the other."

Velvet sucked the frosting off of his fingers. Blagger twitched. He really wished the man wouldn't do things like that. He moved off, calling Honey with a tip of the head. "Anyone else for me?" Blagger asked.

"Not that I can tell with the formality of the dances and all. Perhaps the one in that outrageous silver pantsuit. What is she thinking?"

"That she'll stand out." Blagger narrowed his eyes at her. "Oh, that's just Paulette. She's a designer, I believe. Or plays at it."

"Can you access the database from up here, or do we need to sneak down to the kitchens?"

Blagger wrapped an arm around Spinner's waist and leaned in to whisper in her ear. "I think I can get in from anywhere on the upper levels, if Marsden hasn't changed my access."

Spinner's eyes danced over the crowd once more. She leaned against his side. "Then, access. Sooner better than later."

# CHAPTER 4

Blagger rested against the wall in the servant's passage. The back hall connected the floors with room for the trays and laundry carts to run around the upper levels without impacting the halls the guests got to see. It was cool in the passage and dim, with the smog-shields up. The passage had stairs between floors and a freight elevator that stopped at the kitchens, the laundry and the guest rooms only. It didn't access the lower floors of the Estate. The walls were littered with scrawled writings from the generations of crusts and crumbs that had worked and played in them. There were tips and tricks and the usual gossip spliced in between rambling poems and dirty limericks. The Lady had even pressed her lips to one area and signed it when she was still a newlywed. One of the Pit Crew had sealed the red lip-mark and signature. Blagger touched it briefly for luck every time he had cause to pass it. He was sure that he wasn't the only one. He still looked the part of a Sugar, but he was leaning back, and typing on his datapad. "Alright, here's what we're looking at. I've got a list of rooms and where their Crusts are staying."

"All of them traveling with Crusts?"

"Most of them. There's a load of Crumbs scurrying

around here too. Sleeping wherever they can find a corner. Fauxtoo artists, a cutter, that sort of thing. Got a list of them too. They're scavenging after the party in the evenings. Might be sleeping in the ballroom."

"Wonderful." Spinner snorted. She was using a poster of a band neither of them had heard of as target practice for her kicks. She shadowboxed with the poster while Blagger did the paperwork side of things. "We'll need to take a look at them."

"Think it's one of them that's nabbed the circuit?"

"They'd fit in below floors better."

"True."

Spinner did a delicate high-kick that stopped precisely one centimeter from the surface. "Don't move." She did a flip in place and stopped her kick just above the skin of his arm. She smirked at him. He answered with a rude gesture and returned to his reading. "Let me see the list. Have you gotten anything from Little Miss?"

"She's not back to her room yet. Cameras show her in the ballroom."

"Marsden's probably screaming bloody murder at us." She smiled brightly. "I think the exercise is good for him."

"We'll be lucky if he doesn't restrict us to quarters for a week."

"The Estate would just fall apart. Let's start at the bottom and work our way up."

"The Crusts'll be in their beds."

"No, they'll be at dinner. We need to strike while they're away."

Blagger sighed. She was right. Out from the back passage and back through the ballroom, unless they went down to the laundry. He considered. "Laundry or ballroom?"

"Ballroom. I need to see everything again."

----------

The ballroom was lit only by the distraction screen, which was showing a concert from some randomly collected children. The guests were fixed on the screen. Blagger and Spinner moved around the edge of the room until they were nearly at the other door. Lady Long's eyes tracked them. She raised a brow. Blagger frowned and shook his head. Her shoulders slumped briefly, but then straightened. She lifted her chin and looked deliberately at the screen. That was enough confirmation for Spinner. She grabbed his hand and pulled him along more swiftly. They were back below floor soon enough.

The Pit took up the lower four levels of the Estate. Security and the Butler's staff had the floor above them. The laundry was just above that. The living quarters for the Crusts were above that, with a floor secured for the visiting Crusts. The kitchens were above that, just below the main entertaining floor and the fifteen floors of guest rooms. The Crusts ate in the kitchen area. All of them. That meant that during dinner, the only people who might not be in the kitchen dining room were the people serving the party and security. Neither of whom would bother with the two Crew who were invading their space.

Blagger quickly tapped in his over-ride code to open the lock on the visiting Crust's floor. He bowed and let Spinner go in front of him. He locked the door behind him. It wasn't as though Marsden didn't know where they were or what they were doing after all. "Which rooms?" she asked. He offered her a pair of thin gloves from the dispenser in the hallway. They were for anyone, Estate or visitor, who was going to work on something that demanded no spots. That being said, they also meant no fingerprints when they wanted to have some sort of evidence to present to the Nobs later.

"14, 19, 5, 7, 53, 11, 29, and 90."

"What do you have against order?" she demanded.

"It's boring."

She rolled her eyes. Blagger had the need for new experiences like a top-level sugar—annoying man. She just hoped his boredom wouldn't lead to him leaving the

Estate any time soon. "We'll start with five." She opened the door. It was shaded light purple to reflect that it was a woman's room. The visitor's rooms were changed as the visitor was placed into the system. Women were light purple. Men were light green. And married couples were light blue. Those who played the line were free to blend those colors. It was mostly to avoid awkward social situations, such as a male servant walking in on a female servant or vice versa. Spinner took a quick walk around the room. There were two twin beds, only one of them in use. Matching nightstands and matching luggage areas. The woman had spread out a simple sleep dress on her bed. Spinner's nose wrinkled as she leaned over the nightstand.

"Don't just stand there looking cute."

Blagger snorted. "I resent that. I am handsome. Not cute."

"In your dreams buddy-boy. Sweet little nose. High cheekbones. Artfully streaked hair. You, my dear, are cute." She moved quickly through what was in the nightstand. Blagger blocked the door open and did a quick, but thorough toss of her trunk.

"Spin."

She was at his side in an instant. Her fingers moved through the fabric, quickly. She found the silk dress that was hidden near the bottom and the jewelry that was in the hidden drawer. "Could be her mistress', but I don't think so," she said. She frowned at the fabric. "Not our thief though. Someone else who can blend in when she's needed."

"Right." He repacked her trunk so that she'd have no knowledge of his presence.

The next two rooms, one female, one male, held no surprises. "Cute sandals," Spinner commented, holding up a pair of strappy gold sandals. "Thought the door was green."

"That means nothing."

"True." She frowned. "This one's hiding something,

but it's from his master, not us. Let's move on."

The next room was a married couple. "You get left, I get right?"

"Then we'll trade up." Spinner dove into the trunk with enthusiasm. This was what she'd trained for when she'd left the Amsterdam for the Berlin. She just couldn't stay in the public eye that working on the security team would necessitate. No the Pit was safer, just not interesting. Blagger turned to the trunk. It was filled with soiled linens and crumpled missives from their master. He frowned. He flattened one of the pieces of paper. So few people still used paper. He scanned the documents with his datapad.

Spinner made a small sound in the back of her throat. "Oh," she murmured. She held up a small toolkit that made Blagger wince. "Would you look at this. Is this what I think it is?"

"A way to make a really big problem? Yes, yes it is." Blagger crossed the room. He offered the papers and took the kit to inspect it more closely. It was a medical kit on first inspection, but they both knew better than that. The green fluid in the jar labeled with some false medication was more than just water with coloring. It was stable enough while it was separated from the blue liquid next to it, but a bit of combining, using the needles in the case meant a rather useful boom. "Looks like a standard lock kit. This could blow open almost anything you come across on an estate."

Spinner glanced at the flattened pages. "These are in code. It'll take me a few minutes to read them. You scanned them?"

"I did. Let me put them back. You put this away." She carefully blocked up the needles with part of the case. They'd think it was clumsiness, not sabotage. Sweet mother, at least she hoped so.

----------

Blagger left everything as he'd found it. His fingers itched to take the little lock-blast kit. His own had been tapped out in his flight to the Estate. He hadn't even been sure he'd make it to somewhat safe ground from the London. His little roadster had barely made it out and away before the O'Hanlan Estate blew. He'd still do the same if he had a chance to do it over. Lady Long had welcomed him with open arms and a week long probation.

The next room turned up a rather extensive jewelry collection. "Are these real?" Spinner narrowed her eyes at them, looking through some other spectrum.

Blagger lifted a strand of glittering white stones to the light. "Every one of them, except for this one. This one's paste."

"Think the mistress knows?"

"That it's paste? Probably. Likely she got it just because it looked nice. Or perhaps to wear when she's in the city."

Spinner snorted. "Or it's been substituted and she'd none the wiser. Smart thief if it was."

"Complicates things," he commented, running a string of pearls through his fingers. "Better if the hue and cry goes up. You can slip so many things out when people are panicked."

Spinner considered that. "I never thought of using an investigation as a cover. I suppose it is a lovely distraction. Let's move on." She repacked the jewelry. Her fingers lingered lovingly on a simple star of fire opals. Blagger noted the style. Yule was coming eventually. And the day he'd declared was her birthday would be in another month. Maybe he could convince Mel to make him something if he handed her the design.

The next two rooms were men. The first one had nothing of interest. The second one though, made Spinner pause at the door. The room was spotless. The trunk was tightly packed. Blagger's brows rose. "Military training or mental?"

"Can't it be both?" She carefully looked through the side table.

He shrugged. He poked through the trunk carefully

memorizing the order. He pulled out a small black pad. It was protected by a password. He shook his head. He synced his own pad to it and copied the encrypted files. He'd break into them later. He put it back where it had been. He frowned. There was no way to make things neat enough that he wouldn't notice. They'd do the best they could.

"One more room," he said.

"Good. Then, we can move upstairs."

"Possibly our thief. Or a thief or two. Definitely people the Nobs would love to bother, but not ours. Or at least, not that I can tell from the servants. Fifty-Three is the only one I'd worry about, but he's dispassionate."

"So, as a threat or a mission, perhaps."

"Perhaps. Doesn't sit well with me."

"Last room." The last room turned up nothing interesting.

Blagger's pad vibrated. He pulled it free. The list from Little Miss had come through. He recognized two names on it as career thieves that specialized in jewelry. Perhaps they had gotten into the jewelry at the last stop. They wouldn't be stupid enough to steal something at the Long Estate. Lord Long would castrate them. Everyone knew that. There were two more specializing in trinkets and blackmail. That left five people he didn't know. "Spin, take a look at this list. Anyone you know?"

Spinner took the pad. She leaned against the cool painted blue wall. It had been pink last year and several before that, but there was spare blue paint from the ballroom remodeling, so they'd used it to freshen up the guest quarters. Impressions meant everything in the Sugar's world. Dirty or run down Crust quarters were as dismaying as running out of food for the party.

"I recognize Randy."

"I should hope so. He's amazing. Did you hear about the Quartermass Estate? He took the whole thing out from under them. They didn't even realize they were signing the papers. What name is he under?" He looked over her shoulder.

"Dynar. He's traveling without a valet. Why would he draw attention to himself that way?"

"Unless he's drawing attention away from someone else."

"Good point." She poured over the list for a minute more. "Let's finish our searches. Can you pull up the upstairs rooms we need to check?"

"Ignoring Randy, Blensham, Handsome, Lucky, and Sweetbelle?"

Spinner nodded. "Sweetbelle? Really?"

"She's very good at what she does."

"She's bitter as a lemon and sharper than my knife."

"Anyone's sharper than that old thing. You need to let me at it." She stuck her tongue out at him. "Room 100 and 101 for the next two. The other two aren't traveling with Crusts either. New fashion you think?"

She shrugged. "Possibly. I haven't heard of it. Might have let them go at the last Estate or they ran off before the end of the Season." She moved down the corridor toward number 100. "Did the Crew get the room locks taken care of? They've all been changed since last Season right?"

"Security reprogrammed them all. Not hard to over-ride for one of us. And by 'us' I mean the Crew, Security, and half the Crusts working the laundry and kitchens."

"Wonderful. We need to talk to Marsden about that. Get things more restricted. All it'll take is some visiting Crumb or Crust to seduce a kitchen worker and they're in the areas that we want secured."

"Just protect the things within the space you want to protect. The security around here's always been a bit easy to over-ride. No one wants to cross the Lord and Lady."

"I know our staff is smart, it's the visitors I worry about. Someone obviously didn't hear the right gossip. Our Helion is still missing." Spinner stepped into room

100. She wrinkled her nose. "What is that horrible smell?"

Blagger sniffed. "I think it's perfume. Just far more of it than we normally smell at once."

"Whatever it is, I think we should get Marsden to ban it for us." She waved a hand in front of her face. "I'll take the trunk."

Blagger stepped forward. He frowned. "Spinner?"

She looked across the room and down at the sparkling shards of glass. "Someone else is searching."

"No, I think there was a fight in here. There's blood."

"Call up to Nurse. See if she's got her up there." Spinner continued to search through the trunk. Blagger stepped into the hall and used the intercom to call directly to the infirmary.

"Nurse? Have you seen anyone but Mel today?"

"Blagger, you know I can't talk about that."

"Just in general terms."

He could almost hear her thinking. "Mel's the only one I've seen for anything beyond a headache."

"No one bleeding from a cut hand?"

"No."

"None of our visitors?"

"No, there's a doctor traveling with the Season, so they won't be invading my space."

"Thanks, beautiful."

"Flattery will get you, well, a date at least."

Blagger chuckled. He turned off the intercom. "Should I call Gov and get them to look for someone with a cut? Or should I just try to corner the Sugar's traveling doctor?"

"We'll check with the doctor. I want to keep Gov out of this."

"He's head of Security."

"So?" Spinner looked at him with a blank face.

"Most people would say, let him handle this."

"We're better than most people."

"Anything else here?"

Spinner lifted up a bloodstained shirt. "I'm going to go

out on a limb and say that this is something that happens fairly often. Abuse?"

Blagger shrugged. "Or consensual?"

Spinner looked through the bottom of the trunk, searching for a hidden bottom. "There's nothing in here that indicates anything unusual in the way of sex."

"We'll check her mistress' things, yeah? She might keep things herself."

Spinner shrugged. "I wouldn't know how that works. I know if I had a slave, I'd make her keep all the things in working order."

Blagger blinked at the images that brought to mind. "Sweet petal of great delicacy, never say anything like that again. For my own piece of mind."

Her smile was sly. "What's the matter, Blagger? Don't you want me to be happy?"

"I am not answering that question on the grounds that it may get me hurt. I'm going to check out next door."

"I'll be over in a moment."

Blagger frowned at the locked trunk. He took his tool kit out of his belt and carefully opened the lock. He'd have to re-lock it when he was done. There was the top layer of regular clothing. Below that, there was enough Sugar quality clothing to pass. There was a box at the bottom with a stun-gun and a more dangerous gunpowder gun. He didn't know anyone was using those anymore. He shook his head. He was getting soft. He'd had one many years ago, before he'd left London. He lifted out the fake bottom and found five sets of paper each for master and servant. Perhaps they traded out Seasons? He packed them away.

Spinner stepped into the room carefully. "Blagger? I think we may have a problem."

"What's that?"

"105 is supposed to be empty, but it isn't."

His head snapped to her. "And what were you doing in 105?"

"Following my nose."

"Let me repack this. If it's really another body, we'll have to call Gov. There's no way around it." He knew that Gov and Spinner didn't mix, but the head of security did need to know if there were bodies lying about. He knew Spinner's background left her less than fond of Nobs. He hoped that was all it was. He fit everything back into the trunk. He relocked it. He stored away his tools. Spinner was blinking rapidly.

"You've already been in haven't you?"

She nodded. "It's not pretty. She was raped."

"Mother's blood." He closed his eyes. "Let's have a look then."

# CHAPTER 5

Room 105 was set up with two twin beds like the rest of the Crust rooms. The walls were scrupulously clean, except for the arc of blood that painted across one of them. The woman's body was sprawled out, legs spread, skirt bunched up around her hips. Her hair was long and spread around her head like a halo. Her skin was mottled with bruises. Her eyes were staring up at the ceiling.

"When we find who did this, I want ten minutes alone with him," Spinner said. Tears of rage burned in her eyes. Blagger nodded once, sharply, like the military man he'd never been.

"We'll need Shalita down here with Gov. She can tell us about her." Blagger put on his radio. "Do you want to call it in? You were first on the scene."

"I don't want to talk to Gov. He'll try to deputize me again." Spinner's mouth turned down at the sides. She'd say something nasty if they started fighting tonight. They didn't need the distraction. She slipped her own radio on.

"Sing out, Gov. Sing out, Marsden. Sing out, Shalita. You're needed on the visiting Crust floor. Room 105. Sing out, Nurse."

"Do you need me physically?" Marsden asked.

"Can your cameras see into the room?"

"No."

"Then, yes, we need you down here. We'll need to find Sun-Yi's Sugar too."

"Sing out, Burgundy," Gov stated.

"Here, Boss."

"Find the Sugar Sun-Yi in room 105 was it?"

"She was living in room 100."

"Find the Sugar Sun-Yi room 100 is attached to. Bring her to the security office. I'll speak with her personally. I'm on the way, Blagger."

"I'll find someone to look after Mel," Nurse said.

"Attention all, Penny is in the main office for me," Marsden stated.

"Marsden?" the Lady's voice cut across all the chatter.

"Yes, ma'am?"

"Should we tie things up early tonight?"

"No, thank you kindly. It would be better to keep them under eyes."

"Then, we shall. Kitchens, we'll need additional food up here. And someone round up the crumbs and ask them if any of them are entertainers. Pay them with an actual bed for the night and a meal."

"Yes, ma'am," Shalita stated. "Sing out, Swanson. You take care of the Crumbs. Sing out, Lola. You have control of the Kitchens."

"Swanson, acknowledged."

"Lola, acknowledged."

Spinner leaned against the wall outside the room. Blagger joined her. Their shoulders pressed together. They waited quietly. Her arms were stiff, shoulders tight. She couldn't relax around Marsden and Gov. Neither of them could. Blagger kept his own posture loose with practiced, annoying ease. Her eyes roved along the hallway, searching for any evidence that needed to be marked and kept. He couldn't see anything. The tiles were self-cleaning. There was nothing on them to indicate that there had been any sort of blood on them.

Shalita made it to them first. Her shalwar kameez was a swirl of color against the walls. Her top was a series of light blues and browns. Her pants a darker brown with blue at the ankles. Her dark hair was held back in a careful bun. She'd wrapped a translucent scarf around her hair for working over the stoves. She raised her brows. "Well, I never thought I'd see two of the Crew looking so lovely." Blagger smirked at her, giving her wide hips an appreciative eye. She slapped him gently on the shoulder. "I'm too old for you."

Spinner snorted. "You're still breathing. You're capable of consent. That's pretty much his criteria as far as I can tell."

"And I'm married." She wagged a finger at Blagger. "As you well know."

"I sort of remember a ceremony. Through the hangover."

"I wondered if you'd taken my husband out." She was married to a lovely man who worked in the greenhouses. The Crew had taken it upon themselves to make sure he'd had a second bachelor's party when the Farmers had indicated that they weren't going to provide liquor. The Kitchens had taken care of Shalita. Spinner didn't want to know what they'd done. "What is the emergency?"

"Sun-Yi."

"She wasn't at dinner. I thought she'd taken ill again. She's been ill for a few days, the poor dear. She didn't want to see Nurse. She's been eating a little bread and some soup. What's happened?"

"I think we'd better wait for the rest of the group."

Gov made it to them next. His face was fixed in a nasty scowl. He had Metro with him. "What's wrong?"

Spinner gestured at the door. "Shall we?"

Gov nodded. She opened the door and the wafting perfume and the beginnings of decay hit them sharply. Gov stepped forward. "Jesus." He dropped his head to his chin. "Metro, give me the camera."

"I've got it, Gov. I've seen this sort of thing before." Metro seemed steady. He filmed the room. Spinner pointed out evidence and samples to take. Gov seemed content to let her. He watched the process from the door to keep from contaminating the scene further.

----------

"Sing out, Burgundy."

"The guest and I are headed to your office. I'll bring her some coffee."

"I'll meet you there."

Blagger considered taking off his radio. He didn't want to be listening to the inanity of the running of the Estate right now. Gov glared at him as he lifted his hand to it. "Fine. Not yet." He carefully held his hand out away from his side.

"You can be trained. Marsden and I had a bet."

"I hear that self-immolation is an interesting past-time. You might try it."

Marsden snorted as he came down the hall. He was tall with a shock of black hair that was turning white at the temples. He carried himself with the grace of a fighter. His suit was black and conservative. He carried a bag across his chest that held the emergency over-rides for the estate and copies of all the data on the servers. He'd never trusted in simply using the cloud for back-ups. His left hand still bore traces of the broken hand he'd gotten as a much younger man. He'd been born on the Estate and he'd die there. There was no question of that.

"Talk."

"Crust Sun-Yi is dead. Raped, it looks like," Blagger stated. "There's a secondary site in her room. They fought or struggled there and then, she was dragged over here. Did the cameras see it?"

"I'll have them run back. Sing out, Penny."

"Penny, here."

"Run back the cameras in the visiting Crust hall."

"On it."

Marsden's mouth dipped into a deep frown. He looked into the room. He closed his eyes and took a deep breath. "Sing out, Nurse."

"I'm on the way, Marsden." Her voice was sharp. Marsden winced and rubbed his arm. Blagger quirked a half-smile at him. No one liked upsetting Nurse. She had procedures she could order that just plain hurt. She bustled out of the transporter with her bag. She stepped into the room.

She let out a choked little cry. Somehow, the blood made it worse than Branch's cleanly snapped neck. She took a deep breath and stepped further in. Shalita leaned against the wall and slowly slid down to rest her head on her knees. Blagger sat down next to her and put his arm over her shoulders. She was dry eyed, but her shoulders trembled under his touch. She touched her wedding ring to her lips. "How can people be so cruel?" she murmured.

"I don't know. I just don't know." He watched the activity in the room. Spinner stood in the middle of the mess gesturing at the walls and the trail that led out the door. "If it's any consolation, I don't know how much she was awake for. It seems like she hit her head."

Shalita let out a bitter laugh. "Cold comfort." She shook her head. "I'll see to the staff schedules and set up interviews with everyone. The visitors don't have radios, so they might not be listening in to everything."

"You can use the Crew common if you need to."

"No. I'll separate everyone into tasks and jam in the internal radios. Sing out, Penny, Kitchens going dark except for Butler and Lady over-rides."

"Heard and acknowledged."

Blagger stood and offered his hands. Shalita stood up. She rubbed the small of her back. "I'm getting old," she confided. "And so are you. I know that black is hiding your grey. You don't fool me."

"You wound me." Blagger held a hand to his heart. She

patted his cheek.

"Gov?"

"Go on. I'll have the team up for interviews shortly. Sing out, Burgundy."

"Here, Boss. Her mistress is in the office. I've gotten her some water."

"I'll be up soon. Marsden, Metro."

"Go on. I'll take charge of the scene. Blagger, Spinner, this isn't your concern as soon as Metro has your statements recorded; find that damned circuit." Marsden's shoulders were tight. His voice was sharp. Spinner gave his arm a squeeze as she passed.

Metro nodded at Gov. He chose an unused room and led Spinner to it first. Her statement would take longer, no doubt. She'd seen it twice. Blagger looked into room 100 again. The perfume bottle glittered like an accusation. He looked for any other signal that she'd gotten a chance to fight back. There were tangled sheets and a shoe poked out from under the bed. He glanced back. Was she wearing different shoes? He crossed the hall to check. Yes, she was wearing shoes that matched her dress. The ones under her bed must be the ones she wore when roused in the middle of the night.

"Blagger." His head shot up. He hadn't been aware of drifting off into his thoughts. Marsden's voice was calm. "Your people?"

"Are all in quarters. They'll be drunk by tomorrow and out of the way. They've got orders to not be alone. Which means the commons probably looks like an orgy by now."

The butler snorted. "Make sure they're sorted. Use anyone you need to to find this thing. Sneak them up the back hall through the Kitchens if you need to."

"Shalita won't like that. And I don't know if I can get them clean enough not to freak out the Sugars. Can I commandeer a few of the maids? They'll know more about the Sugars than they know about themselves."

"Visiting or ours? Visitors are only nominally under my

control."

"Visiting and ours. I'll ask the visitors my questions after Gov's crew gets through with them. Let them think I'm some Sugar playing at detective."

"Don't do anything I'll have to report."

"You know me better'n that." Blagger gave Marsden a sweet, lying smile. It made him look a little dimmer and nicer. Marsden shook his head.

"What did I do in a past life to have to deal with you on my staff?"

"You were very good to a lady."

Marsden snorted. "I should have told the Lady to throw you off the Estate. No matter how good you are with your hands."

Blagger smirked. "We'll make you Crew yet."

"Oh, shut it." Marsden shook his head, but his shoulders had relaxed. Blagger took his turn with Metro.

# CHAPTER 6

"Well look at you two," Tread smirked. "Looking like right Sugars. Like something that needs to get a little dirty."

Spinner shook her head. "Oh, Tread, I'll clean you up and parade you around the upper floors some day. I think you'll be fine. Stopped in for a drink. And to see if one of you pigs can be cleaned up enough for upper level work."

Tread cocked his head to the side. "We doing a full-scale search then?"

"I've got a few specialized searches that Blag and I will handle, but I need people to look at the back halls."

"You lot sober enough to not do something stupid?" Blagger put in. He studied each face in turn. They were scared, they were grieving. But there was a strength in them that the Crusts and Sugars would never understand. The Estate was theirs to control, protect, correct, steer, and fix. They loved her with every fiber of themselves. He nodded. "Let me parcel out search parameters. No one goes alone. Teams of two."

"Count me out," Warder said. "Nurse said I need to not use my eyes for the rest of the day while the treatment takes."

"Tread, you staying with him or teaming up with someone else?"

"I'll stay with him," Ham said. He tapped his leg. "I need to let this knee rest up for awhile. Maybe tomorrow."

"There you have it. I'll go with Euclid then." Tread nodded. Blagger nodded. He swiftly divided the back floors for searching and sent out the assignments. "We're looking for the Helion?"

"Remember it's the ugliest green possible. Try not to get anything dirty. Anything we dirty up, we have to clean up during the maintenance sweeps after the party. And if we don't find this thing, we're going to be pushing off blind and hoping like Hell that everyone can get out of our way when London drops our line."

Tread swallowed hard. "So that's a sure thing?"

"Marsden got the communication."

"We'll search. And then, after we get it installed and get the Hell out of the way, we're all getting smashed. Who's with me." The entire Crew raised their hands.

"There better not be any emergencies tomorrow. Spinner and I will be off radio. Call for Penny or Velvet or Honey. They'll be able to get a message to us."

The team took a look at their assignments. Soon enough the room was empty. Blagger sang out, "Blagger, here. Going off radio."

"Heard," Penny told him. He tucked the radio into his pocket. He leaned his forehead against the wall, careful not to touch it with his white shirt. He knew what the walls down here collected. Spinner tucked her hand into his. He gave it a squeeze.

"Let's go, Blagger. There's a thief to find. And two murderers to deal with."

"Right. Tell me we can do this."

"We can do this. First the thief. Then, the jerk who killed Sun-Yi. If Gov and his team hasn't found him yet." Her voice was cold. He straightened his shoulders. He looked her in the eye and saw no hesitation there.

"Tell me, were you a Nob?"

"Don't be insulting, Blagger. Do I look like a Nob?"

"Military Nob maybe." He considered. "But then, you wouldn't be so useful if you were a Nob."

She shook her head. "Let's go find ourselves a thief, and clear some suspects of murder."

Blagger spun her out and back to him as they left the transporter. They slipped into the increasingly drunk crowd and slipped up to Little Miss. She slid her key into Blagger's pocket as he passed and tapped it twice. He gave her a shallow nod.

They'd meet her in her room in two hours.

He set the transporter to take them to the middle 11th floor, just to annoy Spinner. He could keep track of the levels.

"11th. Truly? You couldn't start on the first floor and work up? Or at the top and move down? This explains so much about you."

"The ships dock on eleven," he pointed out reasonably. "At least all the little ones. We can savage one of the steering circuits. Maybe. It'd be an ugly patch job." He stopped dead, staring at the small vehicles. "Brooding saints."

----------

Spinner stood in the middle of the room and turned in a slow circle. "There's cameras here. Lots of cameras. How did this happen?"

Every single ship had its front access panel open. She couldn't tell what was damaged, but there was no way that anyone would be running quickly. He frowned. "This doesn't make any sense. Why take the Helion and not leave yourself a way to escape?" Blagger asked.

Spinner was very quiet. "Because you're willing to sacrifice everything." She'd do it, if she had no other choice. Some targets had collateral damage.

He stared at her. "Everything. To what end? What good could come of something like this?"

"The people in that ballroom are the top of the top. They're the rich ones who don't need to work. They're the ones who make alliances. They're the fops and people who party to be seen. If you destroy them what do you have?"

"A bunch of people who take their place. It's just an accident."

"But if we crash into the London? What would an Estate this size do to London?" Her voice was as calm as if she were reciting statistics. "Come on, Blagger." She could see his thief's brain turning off and his strategist kick in.

He narrowed his eyes at her. "Stars and moons," he murmured. "If the Long hits the London full stop, it'll take out the front. The Estate won't crumple like the newer ones. It'll open the city to the smog and destroy the environments on the farming levels." He swallowed hard. "If the crops fail, the crusts and crumbs are the first to go. It'll be a slaughter-house if the crumbs and spice start fighting."

"And they will fight. The thieves and the con artists and the mercenaries. All the villains of the piece will start to fight. They want to survive and the Sugars are helpless against that. On top of that, the Long Estate. With the Lord and Lady being some of ours?" Spinner's voice was calm almost cold through years of practice. The Longs were hers to protect now.

Blagger closed his eyes. The Cities had a fragile balance. There was just enough food to go around most days. More on the upper decks where the Sugars were hiding themselves. But still not enough, even for the Sugars. That's why they traveled the Estates in this never-ending round of parties and deals in the guest rooms. The Crumbs wouldn't take kindly to it if the Sugars tried to take more than their share and they were sure to try.

And if London went, Amsterdam would have to take survivors and they couldn't afford that. And so it would go. Cities limping and locking together. Estates dangling around them like satellites around a planet. It would even out, but it would hurt. And it would hurt badly.

"Who benefits?" His voice was a croak.

Spinner barked out a sharp laugh. "The religions, of course."

He frowned. "Not most of the ones I know. Fear increases membership of course, but that's not what you're talking about."

"The Religions. That's what they call themselves. At least they did when I left that training on Chicago."

Blagger didn't keep up with politics as much as he ought and it was beginning to show. "The Religions," he parroted. Spinner gave him a moment to think. She raised one brow in question. His face paled. "Mother of Cheops. Those bits who think that we should make planet-fall and try to live off the land again? Those Religions? The ones who think that's in any way sustainable?"

"They don't care if people starve to death as long as they do it in the right way." She traced the design on her collar-bone. "They want to lose the technology and go back to the old way of life. If they have an agent here, they'll sacrifice themselves."

Blagger shook his head. "And how would they be hiding in this society. How could they stand it?"

"True believers will do almost anything. I've seen it happen. I've seen people walk into rooms with explosives and not walk back out." Her eyes were very far away. "We can't let people die here."

Blagger frowned. He put his radio on. "Sing out, Penny."

"Penny, here."

"Roll back tape on the dock. I need to know who's done the damage I see here. Crew, sing out. Blagger needs you at the dock on 11. Bring tools. We have ships to fix. About 450 to fix, minimum."

"Blagger, sing out."

"Here, Marsden."

"What's happened?"

"Someone's hurt all the ships. They need fixing. My Crew is on it. Ask Kitchens to bring up late night snacks. Nurse, sing out, we need Mel on the docks."

"She needs to sleep."

"She needs normalcy. Send her to me on the docks," he contradicted. "She'll be with her family and have something to occupy her hands. I'll come get her myself, if I need to."

"I'll bring her up," Metro offered. "I need to get video of what's happened."

"Good enough for me. Nurse?"

"It's her decision."

"Tell her we have 450 ships to fix. At least one of which will need her special talents."

"Boss? I'm here," Mel's voice was sleepy. "Let me shake off the drowsies and I'll be up. I'll bring the welder."

"That's my girl." Blagger's smile stretched across his face. He beamed with almost parental pride. Spinner rolled her eyes. She stalked around the room, looking at each ship and making notes on the pad she'd taken from his pocket. The first Crew members made it to the dock well before Metro.

"Holy Hell, Blagger. What sort of parties did you have here?" Tread punched him in the shoulder.

"Not me. Spinner's doing first analysis. Hold on fixing until Metro gets here and films it. Penny, sing out. What's the status on that film?"

"I've got two people on the screen. Neither one gave me a good shot. Hats and lights. Can't see a blessed thing."

"Male or female? Can you tell?"

"I'd put money on male for both of them. Still no idea beyond that. Wearing black in the film. And gloved up. Smart for all that."

"Any hair color? Send me a scan on my pad?"

"I'll post you a clip."

----------

Blagger listened to the swirling chatter. It was quieter

than normal. The Kitchens were still black. Which meant the Farms were down too. The Crew, Security, and Marsden's team were still talking. He could hear the Lady chatting lightly with her guests. No one seemed ready to leave the party just yet. He closed his eyes and focused enough to hear that Honey was chatting up a new acquaintance. Velvet's voice was absent, but there were sounds from the musical group that was setting up. Gov was talking calmly to Sun-Yi's Sugar.

"Blagger." Spinner snapped her fingers in front of his face. "Where do I start people?"

"Work from the back in. They'll need to be the first ships out." He frowned. "No, start front to back. We don't want anyone just slipping away as soon as the storm clears. And if there's a ship hiding in the group back there, make sure it can't take off."

Spinner shook her head. "No, they were very thorough. There's no way anything in this dock is taking off right now."

Mel snuggled into Blagger's half- hug, pressing her face to his chest. Metro's eyes grew wide as he looked around the room. There was a flash of green as his implants did a rapid count and measured the space. "Mel, will you walk with me and tell me what's happened on each ship for the record?" Metro gave her a small smile.

Mel nodded against Blagger's chest. Then, she straightened her shoulders and led Metro up and down the lines of ships. "Tread, Lantern, I want you to triage the ships. Follow along behind Metro. Correlate the damage to the ship logs and keep track of any and all costs. Spinner's started the work log. Marsden will need to see a record of everything we've done. Divide the room in rows. Work left to right and front to back. If anything's leaking, that takes priority." Lantern gave Blagger a crisp salute, as though he were still in the Army.

Spinner shook her head. "This will take until after the storm clears to fix. Even if we work three shifts."

"Mica, you're in charge of shifts. Make sure everyone takes regular breaks. If they've been up over twenty hours, make sure they sleep for at least four hours before they get their next assignment. Kitchens are going to bring up food. Don't touch any ship that Metro hasn't filmed." Blagger rubbed the bridge of his nose. "Blagger's signing off. Sing out Mica, you're contact."

"Mica here."

"Penny hears."

He tucked his radio away. He sent a quick message to Little Miss. *Won't make the two hour window. Wait up for me, if you can.* "On to the room we were originally headed for?"

"Why would anyone be on the dock level who isn't a pilot?" Spinner's forehead crinkled. "Single?"

"Single and last minute, I'd guess. We'd have to ask Marsden."

"Later. The last thing I really care about is Sugar politics. A bunch of artificial bullcrap."

"Crap can be very helpful in understanding how people act."

Spinner punched him in the arm. "Stop trying to make me follow my own pronouncements."

"Everyone else is too scared. If I don't call you on it, who will? Mel?"

"Mica, maybe. I've got my eye on her. She'd probably make a nice assistant."

"Oh, are you under the impression that you're taking over for me?"

"Lady Long's under that assumption. Has been since I moved into this place."

"Cheeky thing." He gave her a quick squeeze. He glanced down at the flashing Mayday from London. He flicked it open as they walked. It didn't give him much more information than that there was damage to the tethers and the Long Estate needed to move. Well, they'd have to wait until the Long Estate had a damned Helion Circuit wouldn't they?

# CHAPTER 7

The dock door closed and the hallway was strangely silent. Blagger suppressed a shiver. He'd gone for years without someone in his ear at all times. But somehow, this wasn't like London at all. The hallway was plush with self-cleaning red carpeting. The walls were a warm pink with stenciled detailing that on closer inspection was lit with tiny lights as you neared it. The doors of the rooms were deep, rich wood tones. A small plaque next to each door showed the number of the room and the name of the person or family assigned to it.

The Ramsey's were in the first room and he raised a brow. If he remembered correctly, the Ramsey's were a new family to the Season. They had a small child with them. It made sense. There was quick access to the docks if they needed to depart. And there was a short walk to the transporter that would take them to the second entertaining floor. There was a child care facility there, staffed with tutors and child minders.

They were the only family on the floor, however. Three doors down from them, on the right was the door they needed—Roseburg. Blagger's over-ride key made quick work of the door lock. He held it open and Spinner stepped in first. He stepped in behind her and closed the door.

The room was small, for a Sugar space. There was a king sized bed in the center of the left-hand wall. Heavy drapes of silver and blue fell from the ceiling and could be used to block the bed off from everything else in the room. A single large window made up the wall opposite the door. Just inside the door to the right was the Sanitizer. To the left was the walk-in closet. On the right hand wall, there was a desk and chair. A crystal chandelier hung from the center of the ceiling, throwing sparkling light across the soft blue walls and the soft blue carpeting. A circular throw rug indicated where the holo-vid would show. An armchair covered in blue brocade sat half-facing the window and the table that was stationed there for lunch.

"I'll take the closet. You look under the bed."

Blagger nodded. He dropped to his knees. The heavy comforter flipped up, exposing a storage area, filled with three flat suitcases. He pulled out the first one and found a standard option datapad, a small printer, and a stack of papers that he couldn't read. They were likely encrypted as his Crust's were. He made a record of the machine and decided to try hacking into it when Roseburg next joined the system. The next bag exposed a stun-gun and a military issue rifle that had been broken down. There were three knives and the carrying sheathes. The imprint of the foam indicated that Roseburg was carrying a gun and a knife with him.

"I don't think he's actually left the service," he called to Spinner.

"He has sheaths sewn into every piece of clothing. How many knives can one man carry?"

"I used to carry seven, myself. I knew a boy who carried no fewer than ten once."

"The most I've ever carried was two."

"Luv, you don't need knives."

She laughed. "True."

The last bag was a bag of personal effects. There was a picture frame. It cycled through a series of pictures of his family, friends, and squad-mates. There were a few more interesting pictures that popped up. Blagger copied them over onto his pad.

"Did you find his porn?" Spinner poked her head out of the closet. "You've suddenly become very quiet."

"I will not comment on that."

"Prude."

"My mum would have my head."

"I've yet to be convinced that you have a mother."

Blagger chuckled. "I was created you mean? I've heard that. I am not a sex-bot."

"Too bad. I could rent you out if you were."

He flipped through the small book that Roseburg carried. It seemed to be in cipher as well. He packed everything back into its appropriate space and fixed the bed linens. The room was clean and neat. There were no personal items on display. The Crusts must be beside themselves at not being able to gossip more fully about him. He moved on to the chair and the table. There was nothing hidden under the cushions or secured under the table-top. It was almost disappointing.

Spinner settled at the desk. She ran the tracking over-ride on the imbedded system. Blagger read the list of sites over her shoulder. "He must be using his own link-up somehow. He's not receiving anything through this machine."

"I've got a tag on it. I'll see what I can find later. Anything we can use?"

"He likes women?"

"Great. So you can distract him?"

"In your very tiny dreams. Did you find anything?"

"Nothing we can use right now. No circuit. No indication that he'd even know where to find it. And until I decrypt his correspondence we won't know if he has a need for it. I'd rather not be in here when he gets back."

"Gov won't let anyone out of the ballroom right now. He'll want to keep them safe, dumb, and happy."

"He'll do what he can, but he hasn't locked down the transporters."

"Maybe we should. You can, right? Tell everyone there's an emergency that's taken them off-line?"

Blagger considered. "Lady won't like that one bit. It'll be a loss of face. The damage in the docks is bad enough."

"Well, then, we're locking down the transporters until we finish the initial investigation of the damage on the docks."

"We can send out a small message saying that there's been an incident on the dock and we need to restrict access to the transporters until it's been resolved. Let them think there's been a spill?"

Spinner nodded. He curled one of her ringlets around his finger.

"You are a very dangerous person."

"I just don't bother to lull people into a false sense of security." She put on her radio. "Penny, sing out."

Blagger put his radio into place. He quietly ordered the over-ride of the transporters.

"Spinner? I hear you. Did something happen to your boy-toy?" Penny's voice was bright and teasing.

"Negative. We need to shut down the transporters for a few minutes. Until we have the situation on the docks contained. Can you let the Lady know that we'll have the issue resolved as quickly as possible."

"Is there a leak?"

"We need to make that determination before we let people upstairs," Spinner answered.

Blagger winked at her. That was a politic answer.

"Right. Lady Long, sing out."

"I've heard. Go ahead, Penny. We'll put up a small notice. Blagger, sing out."

"I'm on it, ma'am," he assured. "Shard, sing out."

"Shard here."

"I need a notice on the transporters. The transporters are closed pending the resolution of a situation on the dock."

"Right. I'll have it up in a tick."

"Blagger, going off-line."

"Spinner, going off-line."

"Heard and heard," Penny stated.

"Okay, so we have a bit of maneuvering room. What's the time until the London decides to make us part of them?"

Blagger opened the back of his pocket-watch to see the actual clock-face. "We've got 32 hours left."

"It's been that long already?"

"We'll need a good two hours to have the circuit back into place or to hit a blind forward or backward through. We'll hope for the best."

"I do not want to explain to Lady Long that we destroyed her Estate." Spinner swallowed hard. "Can you imagine what she'd do?"

"Drop us off the dock, I imagine." He kept his voice mild. Spinner shoved at him.

"Brat."

"It's not like she'll shoot us. That would be a waste of money."

"Very funny."

"And knives are so messy. There'd be costs involved in that as well. No, much better to drop up off the dock. Get caught up in the engines though." He tapped his lip.

"So there's nothing here except things you can't read. You see if you can crack his code. I'll lead you to the next room. Which is?"

"978."

"Name?"

"Swinton. The one who was in the white and purple dress who was off to see her Crust."

"The short one with the hair that matched her dress?"

"Yes." Blagger focused on his datapad and let Spinner lead him through the halls by the pocket of his vest.

# CHAPTER 8

The only difference on the ninth floor was the pattern on the walls. Room 978 was done in the same blues, but in the reverse configuration. "I get the closet this time, then?" Blagger raised his brows.

"Indeed." Spinner ducked into the main room and started under the bed. Blagger stepped into the closet. He ran his fingers over the variety of textures of her dresses with a sad smile. He'd never be able to get Spinner to agree to something like this. She had three dresses and one formal pant-suit. He'd been trying for years for her to let him modify discards for her, but she refused every time. Well, maybe he'd make something for Mel.

There was a range of purples, all of which had white accents. There was room in the back of most of her dresses for a sap or expandable stick of some sort. He wasn't sure if she carried an electrified one or not. Her shoes were mostly flat with sensible cushioning. There was one pair of taller shoes with support for her ankles. She might be able to fight in them as well as Spinner could, but she obviously didn't prefer to.

There was a small, locked box that he quickly opened. A few real pieces glittered among the paste. He nodded to himself. She had a copper wire for her hair, but it was the rarity of the gold star of purple gems that made him pause. He lifted it up. Nearly 700 years old, if he was right. The stones were rich and clear amethyst. His heart beat a little faster. "Spin, come look at this."

She put her head in. "Something we can use?"

"No, just something to see."

Her face softened. She touched the edge with a reverent finger. "It's lovely. Now, put it back and get back to work." She tugged on a bit of his hair.

"Right. Slaver." He put it back into place and relocked the box. The next box was filled with bits and pieces that could be assembled into something to hold back her hair. There was nothing in there that looked as though it had come from the Helion. He closed it up. He moved to the next box. Nothing but lacy underthings. He appreciated one of the white undergarments for a moment. Maybe on Shaunna down in Farms. It'd contrast nicely with the warmth of her skin. He shook his head and packed everything back away.

He checked the pockets of her traveling jacket carefully. There were the usual emergency supplies. Small resistors and a coil of wire to fix the internal systems of her ship when they broke. She was the pilot then. A familiar hand poked through the door and snapped twice. "Let me have your datapad." He placed it into Spinner's hand. Her hand retreated out of the closet. He shook his head with a fond smile.

"I'm adding a pocket to that dress," he called out.

"Touch my dress and I'll steal your pocket-watch"

"Evil woman."

"Actions have consequences," she sing-songed back. "I haven't gotten to the desk yet," she told him as he joined her in the main room.

"I'll check on her system logs." He pulled them up. A quick scan didn't turn up anything unusual. "Nothing I see. She's been looking for a mate for a quick pick-me-up, but there's nothing come back yet."

"She's using the internal messaging system for that?"

"No, the Sugar lists. Great places to make arrangements those."

"The Sugar lists?" Spinner cocked her head to the side. "I haven't heard of those."

He blinked at her. "They're controlled, sort of. Only supposed to be for people traveling with the Season. Following on a server that's run by one of the Crumbs. It's a place to make arrangements or let people know which room you're holding a salon in." He shrugged. "I used it occasionally to make arrangements of my own." He smirked at her. "They never seemed to mind and I usually got a few trinkets or a credit out of it."

"Would someone like Little Miss be using it?"

"Oh, no, she's a professional. There's rules about that sort of thing."

Spinner looked at him flatly for a long moment. "So you weren't? I always thought, well, it's just that..." she trailed off. She frowned trying to slot the information into place.

"I worked with Randy for a little while, but I've never had the stomach for long-term games like he runs. I've got an eye for jewelry and other useful bits." His stomach twisted a bit. It wasn't a lie exactly, but it wasn't the whole truth. Randy had been one of the best at using his lovers for wealth and power. He'd been running a love-con on one of the last Season events they'd held at the Long's. He'd caught a glimpse of Blagger and tried to start up their association again, but Blagger'd lost his taste for manipulating lovers years ago.

----------

"That intrigues me. And the Lady?"

"Is perfectly aware of my past." Blagger smiled and it crinkled up his eyes. It wasn't his real smile which was always fleeting. "She is a brilliant judge of character, you know. Now, you don't get to ask anything more unless I get the answer to a few of my questions."

Spinner nodded sharply. "I trust the Lady's judgment of course. Besides, I know you're enjoying the crew. You wouldn't stay if you didn't."

"And I'm the only person you trust not to do something unsavory."

She blinked. It was true. He'd taken one look at her and figured out that she didn't want sex. It was more than most managed.

"I guess, I mean, I trust you," she said finally. "You're my partner. I wouldn't keep you otherwise. It wouldn't even be hard to set up an accident." She smirked. "You wouldn't even know it was me."

"Oh, Spin, I'll always know when you decided to kill me. I read people too, you remember. Not as well as you do. And wouldn't I love to know where you learned that, but when you decide to kill me, you'll give me fair warning."

True, she admitted to herself. "I suppose. Now, there's a stun-stick under the pillow on the bed. And I'm pretty sure she's been storing something else along the side board. No circuit."

"She'd know what it is though. Her traveling coat makes me think she's the pilot."

Spinner nodded at that. "I'm fairly certain she's letting her Crust spend the nights with her too."

"That's interesting, but not that abnormal. They probably protect each other." He shrugged. "Not unheard of the closeness being a little more than just trust too. I'll put my ear to the ground as see what the chatter is in the Crusts."

Spinner looked around the room one last time. "Next one on the list?"

"1266."

"Order, Blagger. It's not a nasty word."

"Just because you don't see the order, doesn't mean it's not there." He sniffed at her.

"If there were any sort of pattern, you wouldn't feed them to me this way."

"Does your mind good to be challenged."

"Challenged does not mean annoyed. You should look it up."

"Right. Let me work on those codes while we walk then."

Spinner snorted. "If you break military encryption while we're walking, I'll have to register you as a national asset."

"Something you want to tell me, sweetheart?"

"Just walk."

----------

Blagger immersed himself in the cryptology. He set his programs running against the files. He wasn't the best in the world, but he was better than most when it came to sneaking into places he shouldn't be. He'd learned coding at the knee of an old discarded man in the lower levels of London. He'd gone by Brand, but his real name was something more interesting. Blagger had discovered it just after the man died, but he wasn't about to let the idiots who'd dropped him ever find out his secrets. It hadn't kept the corporation from coming after him, but he'd kept them at bay. Lady Harrington had made the Welkstet Corporation one of her targets and it hadn't taken long to subsume them into the family's interests. He might possibly have shown her a few secrets along with providing her ribbon roses.

He found a thread and followed it, not watching where he was headed except to react to the pressure from one side to the other as Spinner turned him. "Where's that card?" She poked her fingers into his pocket, looking for the key. She opened the room. "Shiva," she murmured. "It looks like a whirlwind hit this place."

Blagger lifted his head. "Well, I don't think he'll notice slight variations quite as much."

"You get the main room. I'm taking this closet."

"His closet's on the floor."

"Oh, you'll be able to sort it all out, I'm sure."

The twelfth floor rooms were half-again the size of the levels below them. They were still all done in the blue that had been discounted when Marsden had bought it. It wasn't fashionable then, but that was then, and now it was the height of fashion. It made the Lady look like a leader in fashion. And he supposed she was. She was the first one to do up the guest rooms in blue and silver. The extra space was used to support an extra chair and card table that could be moved to the center of the room. There was a stack of folding chairs made of true wood to go with it. He cocked his head to the side. It looked as though they'd actually been used.

Millipede was a gambler perhaps. That would be an interesting game to sit in on. Blagger picked is way through the clothing splattered across the floor. Couldn't decide on what to wear, that was obvious. He wondered if it were an attempt to impress someone in particular. He checked under the bed and found the traveling bag. Everyone seemed to store their datapad and accessories there. He flipped it open to find something more incredible. It was a full toolkit for creating watches. Old school watches. Blagger's fingers itched to try the tools out. He wanted real equipment designed for fixing pocket-watches. His improvised tools just didn't always work.

He closed the toolkit and lifted it out of the way to see what was beneath it. There was no Helion circuit. There wasn't even a datapad. There was an old-fashioned book, bound with real cowhide. Blagger's breath caught. He hadn't seen one of those outside the most expensive collections. He very carefully replaced everything. He found the datapad under the pillow on the floor. He shook his head. He broke the password easily with the author's name. Anyone willing to spend the amount necessary to get a bound copy of Doyle's work would obviously be obsessive enough to use it as a password.

He scanned the anemic number of files. He opened a likely looking spreadsheet and whistled softly. "What is it?" Spinner popped her head out of the closet.

"The man is... This is an unnecessary amount of money. He could buy and sell this Estate and likely the Scrubbs and the Tryoles while he was at it. Hell, he could probably take controlling interest in London."

Blagger's instincts twitched to take advantage of the numbers in front of him. A rich hobbyist would be an excellent catch. He shook off the social-climber mind-set as Spinner asked:

"Inherited?"

"Some of it. Some of it is antiquities and collectables. That watch of his? He makes them."

Spinner stared. "The one with the rainbow vest then?"

"Yes."

"*That* knows how to make things?"

"Wouldn't know it by looking."

She shook his head. "I would have sworn he was military."

"There's still a possibility." He kept scanning. "He's not pulling a pension from them at the least."

"He's not carrying any sort of weaponry."

"Then, he's just protective of himself. With good reason."

"Kidnapping is not a good idea."

"No, I just want to see if he'll tune my watch for me." Blagger sighed. He copied over the files and shut down the pad. He slid his hand along the sides of the bed, looking for the weapons that should be there. He found a bound diary. "Whore-son," he muttered. He scanned the pages in for reading later. He continued through the room. He found nothing hidden.

Spinner glanced through his connections on the in-room system. "This is the most boring connector I've ever seen. He's reading books on it."

"Next candidate then?"

"Who is?"

"Richardson. 723."

"Top to bottom or bottom to top, choose one for the love of all that's holy!"

"Can't remember them in that order."

She poked his shoulder. "Fine. Back to your code-breaking." She sniffed. "Unless you think the kids need a check-in?"

"We're finding the circuit. There's no better service."

"Right."

# CHAPTER 9

The pattern of roses that the lights painted only had seven flowers on each repeat. It was easy enough to determine the floors once one caught on to the pattern. "Which one is this?"

"Richardson. Dragon tattoo. Doesn't have a Crust with him."

"And the code?"

"Almost through." He set his pad to keep working without his input. His eyes were almost picking out the code pattern, but the machine could work on it while he put himself to good use. "The dragon tattoo is real by the way."

"How can you tell? It looked like a fauxtoo to me."

"It's actually a corps signal. Dragon like that only gets put on folks with a particular history."

Spinner frowned. "I've never heard of that."

"It's not the sort of thing they advertise." Blagger shifted and rubbed at the back of his neck. "It's for a little bit of a trouble you see. You only get it if you've pulled off a certain type of mission. I learned to read it. I didn't get to see it closely enough to tell if it was just an infiltration or if it were a kill. I'm sure there's something in the color that tells you more."

"You'll have to teach that one to me. I've never had the decoding for that. And just who were you trying separate from their credits who told you about that."

"I was working with a cat-creeper for awhile. He had rules. You didn't mess with Dragon corps."

"Because they're dangerous?"

"Because they deserve to be safe in their homes."

Spinner looked over her shoulder at him. "Really. I didn't take you for a military supporter."

"Most Dragon Corps weren't from the Sugars, you know. Most military isn't. Quickest way to move up, course, but not like they're born into it most of them. And it wasn't my rule. Still isn't. I just remember what they get asked to do."

"And why didn't you join?"

"Needed a sponsor didn't I? And where was I going to get one of those. No, I was better off doing what I've done. I'm a lover, not a killer."

"That's true." Spinner's eyes softened. "I'm not picking on you. Honestly. I just don't like secrets."

"Keep enough of them yourself." He held up a hand. "I'm not asking you to tell me anything. I don't care, sweetheart. I don't. Once you come here, you're Estate and I don't care anymore."

She bit her lip. "We'll talk after we survive this."

"Think positive. That's my girl. I'll get the bed this time, you take the closet." He squeezed her shoulder and offered the grin that always made her eyes roll. She didn't disappoint.

"What sort of things do they do? Tell me a story or two."

"It's all rumors and shadows of course," he warned.

"As though I really believe anything you tell me? I've heard you talk about your conquests for years, after all."

"You wound me." He stepped into the main part of the room and started looking under the bed. He was careful not to touch anything without checking for trip-wires. He carefully disassembled the bombs he found. "Be careful in there. He might have things rigged."

"Are you not telling me something I should know?" she prompted.

"He's very dangerous. He's very paranoid. And he's likely got some sort of security on everything in this room. And he will likely kill us if he finds out that we've invaded his privacy."

"Oh, glory. Then tell me a story."

Blagger picked his way into Richardson's weapons case. "Once upon a time, there was a small little group of military men who were chosen for their flexible morality and their loyalty to the government of London. They were brought into service and could never tell anyone what they had seen or done. They were trained to be deadly and terrifying. They did missions for years and then were freed from their service with a pension and nightmares."

"And the tattoo."

"The tattoo is just before they leave. Last things their mates do for them." He stared into the lovely group of weapons. He stroked along the barrel of the blowgun and then, the knife's blade. "You want to see these before I close them up and re-hide them?"

"Yes." Spinner leaned against his shoulder and looked at them. She whistled low. "I haven't seen one of those in person. I've only ever heard about them." That was actually surprising. Spinner loved weapons.

"That's how it goes for most people." He sighed. Then, he closed the box and relocked it. He placed it back under the bed and reset the alarm. He moved onto the next while Spinner returned to the closet. There was another case filled with the bits and pieces he would need to fix his ship. This one took longer to look through. There was no Helion circuit. He repacked the bits and pieces into their respective layers and relocked it. The rest of the room turned up no surprises. "I'm sure we tripped some sort of alarm or signal that we've been in here."

Spinner nodded. "He had security on his boots. That is a higher level of paranoia than I was ready to believe."

"Onward, I suppose. 345. Hammersmith."

"Male or female?"

"The woman with the black hair and silver earrings. She was wearing the fairy wings in her hair."

"I wonder where she found those. I haven't seen them on anyone else."

"Not from a standard shop. Could be her Crust makes them. Or something like."

"I suppose. How close are you?"

Blagger looked down at the decryption. He blanched. "Oh, I'm closer than the government would like to know." Spinner settled on his arm as they walked. She read over his shoulder with quick glances while he finished up the last of the coding. "I'm in." He scanned through the information as they made their way to the next room. He deleted irrelevant files as he finished them. There was no need to keep that sort of information on the network. He made sure to triple purge them and to over-write them with circuit patterns and pictures of pretty women and men. Those were the sorts of files he was expected to have on his datapad. As long as he didn't sync with the main system until he was done with them, it should be safe enough.

Spinner opened the door. "You get the closet this time."

"Wonderful." He tucked the datapad away with a gnawing sense of relief. There was always information he wished he could unsee on military machines. The closet was more boring than expected. All of her clothing was the same black iridescent material. It shimmered with highlights of blue and purple in the light. She had pant-suits and dresses and even casual clothes, all made of the same material. "Look for evidence of mourning. I can't think why any Sugar would have a wardrobe this blessedly boring otherwise."

"Right," Spinner called back. Her voice was slightly muffled from the bedclothes she was looking under. There was a box of similar fairy wings in rings, hair decorations, and necklaces. There was even what looked to be a full-sized pair in a special protective box on the floor. "She makes the wings. I've found her tool box and raw materials."

Blagger settled at the desk. "Her business, you think? Trying to start her own fashion?"

"Strange hobby? Superstition?" Spinner shot back. She studied the toolkit. "I think it's a hobby. She might sell them, if someone asked for something in particular. But it looks to me as though she just likes making them."

"To each her own." Blagger shrugged. "Oh, she's a widow. Lost him in the service. A fellow Lieutenant who blew up with that supply ship disaster, two years back. She's been rereading his letters." He searched through the rest of her messages. "No liaisons planned for while she's here. Looks as though she's meeting someone at the next Estate, however. A Miranda."

"On the Blackstone Estate? I believe Miranda's their head of security."

"We could ask Gov. He'll likely know. Could be they were in service together." He frowned at the missive. "I'd put money on it actually. They're talking about her husband and the time they got him drunk to get a fauxtoo on his face that he thought was real." Blagger chuckled. "I'll have to remember that. Think I can get Marsden drunk enough?"

"I think he'd drop you off the dock and tell Lady Long you disappeared with one of the Sugars."

"True enough." Blagger smirked. "She might even believe him. Of course, she'd also cover for him if he were sloppy enough to leave evidence."

"I don't believe he could be that sloppy. His head would explode. So, are you going to let me see those files?"

"I don't think so. Not unless I find something relevant. The fewer people who know, the easier it is to keep the secret."

----------

Spinner rolled her eyes. She held her hand out for the datapad and he gave it to her. "I promise not to tell," she said—affecting a little girl voice.

"So long as you never use that voice again, I promise not to call you on the lie."

She scanned through a few of the files. Her brows rose. "Definitely not out of the service. I'd be shocked if he were the one who'd done this though. He works for London doesn't he?"

"That's what it looks like to me." He scrubbed a hand through his hair. "Let me have that back. I need to check the Crew progress before we head on to 1053."

Spinner growled in the back of her throat. "If we had more time, I'd batter you ruthlessly with a pillow until you put these rooms in a proper order."

"I'd suggest seeing Little Miss, but I don't want to open the transporter doors yet. And she won't talk to us on the floor. Not about anything that matters." He took the pad back as they left the room. "He could still be doing this. We can't count him out."

"What gain is there for London?"

"If they need to start a war? Or they want to get aid or create new alliances? Or maybe just to reduce some of the population. If they've got it timed right, they might be able to only harm Crumbs and Spice."

Spinner's hand tightened on his arm. "You say that as though they don't care."

"Maybe it's different in Amsterdam, but in London, if you're not a Sugar or attached to one?" He shrugged. "Scrape by. Scavenge. But you don't count. Not really. You're just considered a waste of resources."

"It's not right."

"And was it any different in Amsterdam?" he pressed.

"No." Her voice was soft. "There were damned good reasons to leave. There were reasons to stay, of course, but the reasons to leave were better."

"More imminent?"

"Consequences. Every action has consequences. And I knew that mine meant leaving. Doesn't mean I ever regret making those choices."

"But if you hadn't?"

"If I hadn't, I wouldn't have come here and that would have been a tragedy. Stop fishing for complements."

"You wouldn't know to compliment someone if there were a sign on their forehead."

"Not true. I compliment Mel all the time."

"She's seventeen and you've been training her since she turned ten. I don't think that counts."

"She's still the best fabricator I've ever met and you think so too."

"Did I say you were wrong? No." He heard his accent slipping. "Hold on, sweetheart. No bickering about Crew or we'll lose character."

She straightened her shoulders. "I'll have you know, that I never lose my character. If you need the help, though."

He pinched her shoulder. "Just for that, I won't modify that dress Mica left for you."

# CHAPTER 10

The crew was making swifter progress on the ships than expected. The saboteurs were clumsy and half of the parts had been left scattered under the ship they'd been pulled from. Blagger sighed in relief. He didn't update the work lists, but he made a note to let the lady know exactly how good his crew had been on their own. "The crew's got 100 of the ships flyable. They haven't found any that were missed."

"And there's no other dock that a visitor could take off from." Spinner shook her head. "They meant to be in the middle of the attack. Whether it's because they don't want suspicion to fall on them or if they're a true believer of some sort is still up in the air." She tapped her teeth as she thought. "No, they've got to be a true believer. Anyone else would need an escape route."

"Unless they thought to take one of the Estate vehicles. We'll need to check them. At the very least, there's the tug. It might be able to get us going in the opposite heading."

Spinner grimaced. "That went down last week, remember? Lady decided that it was more important to keep the guest rooms fixed than to work on the tug."

"Mother of sirens." He groaned. "That's right. What

would I do without you as my memory?"

"Use the datapad and whatever you used to do before I came here."

"That's strange. I can hardly remember what I did do before you came. It feels as though you were always here."

She kissed his cheek. "You're still sweet."

He smiled. They'd never gone beyond a kiss, no matter what everyone seemed to think. And they never would. It wasn't that he thought of her as his sister. Not exactly. She was his partner, his best friend, his better half, and all the other permutations of relationships. He loved her dearly, but he wasn't in love with her. "And this is why the girls keep begging to see your ring."

"Rings are dangerous and would only get in the way of the work. Room 1053 Loisdale. Which one is this?"

"Pink stripes in her hair and on her dress."

"The one with those muscles in her arms that look as though she's been weight training to lift a 1-seater?"

"That's the one."

Spinner nodded. "You find her weapons. I'm going to find out how big her sleeves are."

Blagger sniffed. "That's my girl. Finally, the fashion bug has bitten you. It's relatively painless from here on out."

"Shut it."

Loisdale's weapon was a shoulder-mounted pulse cannon. "Saints of the twin systems. I didn't think they let these wander out of the armories."

"Given I just found her uniform? I'm going out on a limb to say that she's not intending to leave the service. She's in the reserve or some such."

"Should we leave her a note about the paste we found down below floors?"

"If she hasn't noticed, I see no reason to bring it to her attention. It might only embarrass her."

"And you care about that now? It's like seeing a whole new side of you." Blagger closed the box and shoved it back under the bed. The other box there was filled with paste jewels. "Huh. I've a feeling she knows. She might even have a sideline that the service doesn't know about. Which City is she with?"

"Patch indicates Columbine."

"Well, well, well, that fits neatly."

Spinner poked her head out. "The paste is from Columbine. Of course. They've been working on perfecting synthetic jewels for military and industrial use. And she's got either rejects or is attempting to see if anyone notices or cares when she wears them in a social setting. She's born to this. I found a picture of the family home."

"Oh? On Columbine or is she from an Estate?"

"Loisdale Estate is a satellite of Columbine. They get too much of their food from the City still to separate completely. And they don't host grand parties during the season. They're much more likely to host weekending City Sugars."

"You ever been there?"

"I was there once. I didn't care for it. The Crusts were lazy and the master of the house was a prat."

"Don't hold back. I'd love to hear your true opinions. So she's the daughter of the prat?"

"Maybe the military taught her something. She's surely not staying with her family on a regular basis. None of the clothes in here are Columbine made. It's all from New Horsham or Paris."

"Paris. That brings back memories. I got to go there as a boy. Lovely place with so much light."

"It is their specialty. I hear their entire hull is either glass or photo-volts."

"We should consider adding more of the photo-tiles next time we get a few credits. It could only help. No circuit. I'm not even seeing indications that she can change a resistor in her ship."

----------

"Typical. Who's next on your increasingly mind-fracturing list?" There had to be a pattern. Spinner just hadn't found it yet.

"Berkowitz. 629. Brown hair with red highlights and the green snake-skin tie."

The search of Berkowitz's room was boring enough that she couldn't stop yawning. "I didn't think it was possible for one person to have so little interesting about him."

"Most people don't know how to have three identities on hand for emergencies." That was the problem with most sugars—lack of pre-planning. Blagger went back to reading military dispatches. "There's a war in Umbria."

"When isn't there? That's like saying that Kinglit has random malfunctions of their water system."

"True enough." She guided her partner as he studied and deleted classified documents. "1511. Dritz."

Spinner smacked his arm, leaving bruises this time. "Next time we do something like this, please present the information either from top to bottom or bottom to top."

"That's not how my brain works. And if I'd done that, we might not have found the trouble on the docks early enough to do something about it." He lifted his chin with a stubborn pout. Typical.

"How is the Crew doing?" Spinner tugged on the pocket of his vest, leading him down the hall.

"They're doing fine. Your fingers getting restless?"

She snorted. "No, there's a much larger possibility of a fight this way." She stopped, stock still. "You don't think the thief destroyed it?"

"Not possible. Not without a torch. And they couldn't over-ride the smog security to throw it out of a window or off of the dock."

"If we don't find it, we'll need to search the wheel-room They left all of the parts in the dock."

"Call Metro and give him a heads up on the possibility?"

"No, they'll try to call us off. We'll do it, if we don't get anything useful."

"We should tell Penny at least."

"When did you get so dependent on the rest of the staff?" She frowned at him. "Just trust me." She settled against his side and he automatically held her closer. His fingers were cold on her arm.

"We have at least four thieves to look for on top of the Sugars. You remember that? We might need some extra eyes."

"You're getting soft."

Blagger sighed. "Losing my touch. I know. I'll practice more."

"And you'll practice fighting with Gov's staff?"

"Hell no. They'd wipe the floor with me." Blagger shuddered. "I'll train with you. Or maybe one of the Farms."

"Me then. Agreed." She gave him a feral smile as she stepped away and forward.

He stilled, thinking. "Blistered cow herpes, woman. How do you do that?"

"Catch you while you're reading. It's easy. You always agree with what I say when you're distracted. Secret female training methods." She smirked over her shoulder at him. She hit the right button and the transporter lurched just a bit as it took off, then shuddered to a stop. "That's not good."

"Someone's over-riding the system? Or just another damned thing breaking?" Blagger snarled out through clenched teeth.

# CHAPTER 11

Spinner pulled at Blagger's belt. He let her get to his tools, then leaned against the far wall of the transporter. He crossed his ankles and lost himself in the stream of data while Spinner dug into the guts of the system. There were three wars in that London was involved in. The Religion wasn't one of them, but Lancaster was. "Lancaster versus London. Would they be willing to do this?"

"To stop the war or just to get the upper hand?" Spinner didn't look up.

"Either."

"They might. Wait, when did London and Lancaster start fighting? I thought they were allies."

"Not according to what I'm reading right now. Looks as though it's been going on for six months now."

"And you didn't know about it? Sounds like misinformation to me. That's the sort of whisper that doesn't get drowned out."

"I don't know. Haven't been getting regular dispatches the way I used to." He'd have to fix that. His Shadows were getting lax.

"The London government is trying to keep it covered up? Aha! There you are, you little sister of Shiva."

"And there's an indication that Lancaster is objecting to environmental policies on the world stage."

Spinner changed out the faulty receptor. The transporter started back up. She cleaned up the panel. Then, she re-buckled his belt. "Lancaster thinks what? That by opposing the environmental policies they'll be able to increase their profits?"

"There's no analysis here. Just facts." Blagger turned the pad around. Spinner scanned it.

"I don't like it. It feels wrong, if that makes any sort of sense. War should never feel right. But this is just illogical. There's no gain."

"But if they're allied with someone else. Would that make sense?" Blagger chewed on his lip. He thought he'd given up the habit when he was still a teenager, but apparently not. He forced himself to stop. He stared off into the air. Spinner pulled him along to the room. "Lancaster is allies with Dusseldorf right? So, there's gain there."

"If London goes down? The only thing that they export in common is, oh." Spinner stopped in the middle of the hallway. "So this is about the wine harvests?"

"London's not known for wine. Only whiskey and beer."

"And if the grapes failed on Lancaster this year?"

"The grapes did fail. That's why we've been drinking beer. Lady prefers Lancaster wine. She'll drink Tbilisi, but Lancaster is sweeter." Blagger nearly smacked himself in the forehead. "Lancaster needs the money from Dusseldorf. But they don't have nearly enough to support a full out war effort."

Spinner opened the door. She stopped short. "Blag, I think this is alarmed or trapped."

"Well, it's not surprising that more than one person would be paranoid. Let me take a look." He handed the pad over. "Don't delete this file just yet." He looked at the wires. "No, it's just for show. Enough to scare off a casual thief."

"It's not as though the cameras won't be watching."

"We're not security."

"No one who isn't Estate will know that. They'll assume we're undercover like Honey and Velvet."

"Let's get this over with. Closet?"

"Oh, no, I got the closet of the most boring man in the world. You get this one."

"You just like sending me into woman's cabinets."

"How true. Someday I'll convince you to wear a dress and watch Marsden pass out."

Blagger laughed. "He's made of sterner stuff. Besides, he's already seen me in a dress. Lost a bet my first year here."

"To whom?"

"Marsden. No harm done though." It had worked exactly the way he'd planned it after all. Marsden had the opportunity to establish a bit of control or at least feel that way. Blagger got to meet more of the Estate and grow his reputation as someone who was laid back enough to take jokes at his expense.

"There are pictures. Tell me there are pictures. Why has no one ever shown these pictures to me?"

"You have to buy them off of Marsden. He's tight with them."

"I'll just have to think of something to trade."

Dritz's closet was as chaotic as her Crumbs' room was. There was a tangled pile of clothes on the floor. They were meant to be headed to the laundry, he supposed. He fingered the cotton. It had the tell-tale weave from the Virginia. Her uniform was the only thing that was crisply maintained in the entire closet. If he'd had to deal with such lax treatment of his things, he'd be on a tear. Dritz seemed to be laid back. A bit too laid-back.

Spinner made a sound of triumph. He poked his head out to see what she'd found. "She's got something sweet here. A little something to make her relax at night." She sighed. "I haven't had a Ket in years."

"I'm sure we can find some sort of substitute for you."

She frowned at him. "There's nothing quite like those hits." She closed the box. Blagger returned to his perusal of the shoe rack. He didn't find anything but far too many pairs of identical black dancing shoes. He ran his fingers along the back wall, looking for anything out of place. There was nothing.

He moved onto the desk. "She hasn't accessed the system from this pad," he told her. "She must have a linkup that she keeps with her." He pulled out the small drawer and found a tangle of coded messages. He scanned them into his pad. "I'm going to just sit here and work on decrypting. Let me know when you're ready to leave or if you find anything."

"I found something." Spinner said after a few minutes of quiet searching.

"Interesting or useful?"

"It's not the Helion. She's got multiple papers in here. Looks as though she's carrying extra for her Crumbs too. Why's she got two traveling with her?"

Blagger didn't answer the question. He knew Spinner was just thinking aloud. Instead he tracked through the next missives about the growing tensions between Lancaster and London. It was just so senseless. Why would Lancaster put their lives on the line when there was nothing to gain? He stopped the thought. What would London gain by destroying Lancaster? They'd gain tithes from the smaller City. And who would be put into the power position for Lancaster? Frank London? Or maybe it'd be someone who wasn't connected directly to the ruling families. "What does London gain?"

Spinner didn't look up. "Territory. And reduction in tariffs in the Lancaster markets. They're punishingly high on imports."

"Are they then? I didn't know that. It was never my territory. I heard that they still execute smugglers there though."

"I've heard that. It's more likely they turn them."

"Depends on who owns them, I expect." Blagger scowled down at the data. "What I can't figure is whether London is hoping this information gets distributed or if it's real."

"Dritz is from Lancaster." Spinner held up an old photograph. The kind you could only get on Lancaster or Mennon. It was Dritz as a young soldier, her hair shorn to follow her skull, a weapon across her body and a smirking smile as she leaned on the other four members of her team. "I'm going out on a limb to say that two of these people are her Crumbs. We'll need to check to see if she's traveling with a pilot as well."

"Unless one of them's gone and died. If I were a government funded thief who was attempting to create a disaster, where would I hide the circuit I'd stolen?"

"Not in my room. That's certain."

"We'll need any of the cleared Maids to look in the back halls. And we'll need crew to check the registers in every room."

"I'll call Gov about it. We'll have to let them start filtering back to their rooms soon or the Lady will have our heads."

"Green suit is the only one left. Monestra. 481."

"Let me finish this, then I'll talk to Gov as we head back down. Those thieves that Little Miss gave us, where are they?"

"They're on 5,10, 6, 3 and 14. Randy's the one on 14, so I don't think we need to worry about him. And we can take Gov's folks with us on those searches, if we need to."

"We'll do them. No self-respecting thief is going to duck out of the party as soon as the doors open up. Was one of them Sun-Yi's?"

"Yes," Blagger said quietly. "I need to take a listen to that interview."

"She wasn't your responsibility."

"We don't know that. It could be connected. We'll take a listen and decide."

"Anything else in those documents?"

"I have to set my programs at working on the scraps I found here and in her Crust quarters." He set deed to word. Hopefully it wouldn't take too long for there to be some sort of answer.

"She's not our thief."

"Why not?"

"She's here to spy. She needs to keep these people intact or she doesn't have the reputation to move into the next levels."

"But if she's a survivor of the catastrophe? It might be worth the possibility."

"If London hits us or we hit London, we're all dead. It'll destroy our life systems."

"Maybe they weren't counting on the smog." Blagger paused. He swore softly. "We need to see who came straight from London."

"Because they might have done something there as well." Spinner hugged herself. "I came here to get away from this sort of shit."

Blagger reached out a hand, but thought better of it. She didn't dislike being touched, but there was something fragile in her posture right now. "Is it more important to check the last room or for me to fight through the last of the intel?"

"Let me finish searching here. You work on the memos. Then, we'll go to 481."

He nodded sharply at that. She worked through the last two travel cases. One of them turned up parts for the ship. Spinner looked through it carefully. "We should consider charging these folks for the work we're doing. A bit here, a piece there," he commented.

Spinner snorted. "Bad thoughts. We're both on the right side now."

"I'll get the go ahead from the Lady first, then. Or

maybe just Marsden. He's a bit more ruthless than people give him credit for."

"He'd have to be. I think he likes his puppy reputation."

"Puppy?"

"Stop being distracted."

"Right. Reading." Lancaster has advanced on London. She's taken the profits from the last three attempts to overwhelm the City with legal precedents. He frowned. "This is misinformation. There's no way it's not. This is the sort of information you feed to a new recruit to make him happy to die for you."

"Then what's the truth of it?" Spinner didn't look up. That trust made warmth run up his sternum.

"I think it didn't start with Lancaster. The statements are true enough, I think. It's just not the full story. Lancaster's come off the better during the court cases and the official channels, which means the inter-city courts are agreeing with Lancaster. London's in the wrong. I just can't tell if it's started because of external agitation or if it's internal."

"Does it matter?"

"Depends. Are you loyal to either City?"

"I'm loyal to the Estate. To the Longs."

"Then, no it doesn't matter. I don't trust either side, but London was home once." He sighed. More than home, London was his responsibility, if he were being honest, but only the Lady knew that. "By that same statement, I don't want to see anything happen to the innocent people in either city." He turned back to the memos. "Finally," he murmured.

"Something good?"

"Something true, at least. Direct orders for our Master Roseburg." He scanned over the files. "He's under orders to scout the Sugars and find out who supports London. Who they can call on as still loyal. And to secure alliances for the them."

"Well, he'd do that anyway right?"

"Probably."

"Then, we can assume that he's not one to set those same people up for death. Time to move on to our last Sugar."

"Right." They locked up behind themselves. The pad vibrated in his hands. That meant his program had found something. He looked at the Lancaster code. He started to read the quick messages back and forth. "They are all from the same unit. Dritz and her Crusts I mean. The ones below floors are married. The male is the pilot. The female is acting as her personal servant on this gig."

"Meaning the man has plenty of time to scope out all those sorts of things we don't want anyone to know."

"If he's poking his nose into the Kitchens, Shalita's got him either working or assigned to the Farms for now."

"Monestra."

"I've got it." Spinner opened the door. She scowled at the place. "This is a mess. I don't envy his Crust tomorrow. You read. I'll search."

Blagger leaned against the wall of the bathroom. He lost himself in the data. When he looked up again, Spinner was in front of him. She shook her head. "There's nothing. Not even a hidden weapon. What sort of self-respecting Sugar doesn't even carry a stun-gun?"

"A male one?"

"Idiots. On to the thieves. May they have more interesting lives. We'll need to look at their Crusts' rooms."

"Put on your radio. I'm going to talk to Penny. I want you to hear the same thing I do."

# CHAPTER 12

"Penny, sing out."

"I hear you Blagger."

"Playback the discussion Gov had with Sun-Yi's Sugar?"

"That's need to know," Gov broke in. "I need a reason to authorize it."

"We need to know if she's one of our suspects. I have reason to believe she's a professional thief, but not necessarily the one who took our circuit."

"Authorized. Make sure Spinner's on before you do. I only want it played once unless you come down to the office. In fact, why don't you come down and give me a report before you listen. I'll even give you both Stim drinks."

Spinner yawned. "Damn you, Gov. I wasn't sleepy until you said something."

"Can you get some sent up to the crew on the docks? I don't want them staying up too late, but the supervisor might need it," Blagger said.

"We'll be down. We're going to have to let the transporters open soon, or people will be asking about what's happened," Spinner pointed out.

"Right now we've told anyone who's asked that there's been an incident below floors and a leak up on the docks. No one's going anywhere. Lady Long has the Crumbs entertaining. It's one of those things that everyone's going to be talking about. Some sort of magical music session." Gov's scorn was obvious enough that Penny giggled at him.

"You are an old man Gov. There's several good musicians on stage right now. They're just playing around, but the recordings are going to make a mint for them and us if we work it properly. I've got all cameras on in the ballroom and all mikes and radios are openly recording there. There's a small area in the ballroom that's been set up for lounging. One of the Kitchens brought up a small battalion of pillows and blankets and it's causing a bit of stir, but they're happy to stay in the ballrooms."

"Keep eyes for us, Penny. We're looking at two military assets in the crowd and the usual wrong side crew."

"No wrong side is stupid enough to cause trouble when they can't get out." Penny stopped talking for a moment. "Unless it's one of those anarchists. They might cause trouble, but they'd be trying to start a fight right now."

"Leave the investigating to Security."

"Are we Security now?" Blagger asked mildly.

"For the purposes of this investigation, yes. Come report."

"We're on the way. Blagger, signing off."

"Spinner, signing off." They tucked their radios away. "I don't want to go down."

Blagger frowned at her. "I can give you the list for the thieves and do the report myself. But I'd prefer to stay together. I promised that no one would be alone at any time tonight."

"Let me fly free for a few minutes. Tell Gov I'm in the toilet."

"You be careful. And I'll put my radio on 78."

"Gov can listen in to that too." She frowned. "I won't

be more than fifteen minutes. You can stall him that long."

Blagger nodded slowly. "You'll explain it to me later?"

"Of course. I just need to check something while Gov's not looking, okay?"

"Don't do anything stupid. I'll miss you."

"Go away now. I need to do girly things."

Blagger smirked. "Tell her I want pictures."

"You are a disgusting man."

"You wouldn't have me any other way."

----------

The door of the elevator closed behind Blagger. He'd be able to hold Gov's attention well-enough that she felt comfortable slipping away. She stepped into one of the small Lady's alcoves that were scattered throughout the estate. They were small chambers that the Lady could step into in order to deal with Estate business. They were private by design.

Spinner switched to the Lady's private channel. "Lady, sing out."

"Spinner." The sounds of the party dulled as Lady Long stepped into one of the chambers. It was no better than a closet large enough for two. "What have you discovered?"

"Branch was killed by Gov," she said baldly. "The Helion is still missing and unconnected to the death. All four-hundred ships on the dock were damaged. The Crew is repairing them."

"Explain," Lady Long stated.

"He went off radio. He had trace evidence on his arm from the choke hold when he came down to investigate. Also, his fiancée has been stepping out with Branch."

"Can you prove this?"

Spinner sighed. "If I need to take it to the Authorities? Perhaps. To know its true for the purposes of our reaction? I think so." She took a breath. "We don't have any cameras in the steering room."

The lady was quiet for a moment. "I need proof. Gov

has been loyal for many years."

"Yes, ma'am."

"Where is Gov?"

"Emergency planning with Blagger."

The Lady was quiet for a long moment. "And Branch's family?"

"Mel is working with the Crew. There's no danger to her. She doesn't know."

"Motive?"

"His fiancée stepped out with Branch."

"Mother of saints." Lady Long sounded tired. Spinner could almost see her pinching the top of her nose.

"I'm sure we have contingency plans."

"We do." The Lady sighed. "Find the Helion. Everything else can wait until we're safely past this crisis. Do tell Blagger that he needs to find a way for Branch's daughter to be unavailable for awhile."

"Yes, ma'am."

"Long, out."

"Spinner, out."

----------

Blagger made his way down to the security office. It was on the upper floor of the entertaining floors. On the opposite side of the floor from the child care center and school. He sat down on the guest chair without announcing himself. He put his feet up on the desk and read a bit more of the Lancaster communications.

"You spend too much time with Spinner. Where is she?"

"I was told to inform you that she was in the toilet dealing with girly things."

Gov made a face. "That was more information that I really wanted. Stim?" He offered a mug of warm liquid. "Kitchen's been sending up gallons of the stuff to hear them tell it. What's the situation on the dock?"

"You've seen Metro's recordings?"

"No, he's still up there, monitoring the situation on

each craft so that we can give the information to the owners."

"It's bad." Blagger sighed. "You saw the checklist postings right? That's just the tip of the iceberg. Spinner put it up in a few minutes. I'm sure it's longer than when it first went up by now." He put his feet down on the floor and leaned forward. He turned his pad to the dock listings and the pictures he'd taken when he first saw the damage. "There's not a ship that wasn't touched."

Gov scrubbed a hand through his hair. He pinched the bridge of his nose. Blagger carefully didn't react to those tells. The man was tired. That was obvious. There was blood on the cuff of his shirt. Sun-Yi's, most likely. Branch hadn't bled. "There was no damage to our vehicles. The service ones. I had Shalita look for us. She says the tug is still malfunctioning, but the other two are still working. Worst comes to worst, we'll send off the Lord and Lady with as many of the kids as we can shove into them. The escape pods won't do anyone any good if they can't see in the smog to guide themselves to somewhere safe, but we'll put as many as we can into them."

"We've never had a drill on it. We don't have enough time to do that." Blagger checked his counter. "There's a new Mayday from London. The tethers are losing strength and they may cut us loose early. They're starting to drift a bit. Something's hit the stabilizers." He took a deep breath to calm the thudding of his heart. Right now he didn't have time to deal with anything about Branch's death. Bigger emergencies first – the loss of tether and the Helion.

"I thought that was the smog battering them?"

Blagger shook his head. "We've got a little over twenty-four hours before it's time to abandon the Estate. Without the tether or the Helion, we're going to drift into the London and if we do that..."

Gov grimaced. "Marsden is in conference with the Lord and Lady. They'll make the final determination. Give me the straight deal. Is there anything we can do in the last ditch beyond get as many people out as possible?"

"We can just fire the thrusters and throw out a Mayday alarm. It'll move us in the same direction as our last heading." Blagger felt slightly sick. "But if we want to steer? We have to put someone in a sling and send them down to manually move the rudders."

Gov raised his brows. He sipped his Stim and leaned forward. Blagger mirrored his position. "What does that mean?"

"That means we'll likely lose two or more Crew members. That I'll lose the twins or I'll lose," he paused to think, "Mica and Bellows. They're the only ones who could do it without being able to see."

Gov sighed. "I thought when I left the Marines, I wouldn't have to make these sorts of calls again."

Blagger snorted. "Hazards of command. You could've warned me."

"Not the first Crew you've lost."

"No. Not the first people I might be sending to their death either." Blagger let his shoulders slump. "I might be able to do it, but someone has to be in the wheelhouse and using the radar, what little good it'll do. The electrical interference of the storm will make us next to blind on all sensors. We have no external cameras. And we can't open the screen or we'll have a smog leak."

"You could put one of the others in the wheel-room"

"Not after 24 hours putting together the ships on the dock for the hope of saving some of the Sugars too. The Lord and Lady off with the children. If they drop straight down, they should be clear of London passing overhead. There was no one below us when the storm hit. Unless someone's drifted off course, there should still be clearance enough."

"Why can't we drop?"

Blagger paused. "We can't stop before we hit the ground. And we'd have to destroy the safety controls."

"But you could do it."

"I can't be sure that I wouldn't destroy a half-dozen or more of the small ships. And if there is someone below us, they're not going to know it. Mother of mercy preserve us. No, we throw as many people as we can onto the ships, send them straight out of the dock and hope for the best. We can send out the emergency pods with as many of the staff as possible. Kitchens and Farms first. Crew's last out."

Gov closed his eyes. He took off his radio and put it into his drawer. He folded his hands on the top of the desk. "You're talking about suicide."

"If London hits us, we're going to lose life systems. If we don't get the guests and the staff out, this is going to be nothing more than a floating graveyard. And if we can't stuff the crumbs into the ships with the Sugars, then we have a problem. Most of them are taking hoppers from one Estate to another and there's no way to get them in here. My last ditch plan, if we can't find the Helion, is to throw the last of the crew out on the tug."

"Can you make a Helion circuit?"

"If I could, we'd have three back-ups. No, they've got to come from the factory or the system won't accept them. You can't open the case or they stop functioning. If our thief actually knew that, they'd just have opened the case and left it in place. I can't understand why there hasn't been a ransom demand."

"Can we salvage one from one of the Sugar ships?"

"They're too small, or I would have taken the one from that sweet red runner."

"The one with the black stripes? Lovely thing." Gov gave him a partial smile. "So, what you're telling me, is that I've got 24 hours before I need to have everyone off of the ship for the last ditch stupidity. Or I drag even the Crew off then and let the Estate take the hit."

Blagger grimaced. "It's going to kill a lot of people in London. Just so you know."

"How many?"

"Best guess? A few thousand." He laughed, bitter. "Doesn't matter though. Just a bunch of Crumbs and Spice. The Sugars and Crusts'll be in the top levels and the double hulled spaces."

"Blagger?" Gov frowned.

Blagger waved a hand and banished his mood. "London sugar doesn't give a damn for the lower floors. Never did. Never will. Just a drain on resources. Doesn't matter how hard they work or all the crap jobs they do, the uppers don't see us as anything."

Gov shook his head. "You're not there anymore. You're Estate now."

"I don't care what Marsden says about you, you're all-right."

The head of security snorted. "Is she giving us privacy to talk about this?"

"Probably. I'm sure she knows what I've been thinking about when I'm not talking to her. Want the run down?"

"Give me the highlights."

"Spin found a list of faces in the ballroom. I ran through the dossiers that the Crusts keep. We paid a visit to the Crusts of the Sugars and found Sun-Yi. Before that though, we found military secrets, a lock-blast kit, paste jewelry, a stun-gun, a powder-gun, and fake papers. No circuit," Blagger stated

"Up in the Sugar space, we found the damage in the docks. Two active military assets. One from Lancaster. One from London. A dragon corps member. And I've got word of five thieves I don't know well enough to discount on the circuit. We're off to check those rooms as soon as we hear the recording of the interview."

"The interview is that important to you?"

"We need to know. Sun-Yi's death may not be connected, but it may well be. We need to hear it. We've been off radio or we'd have listened in."

"And what did you find with the military assets?"

"They're our best suspects, but I'm sorting through intel." Blagger sipped his Stim as he thought. "There's nothing yet. We'll need Security to help us with the search on the entertaining levels and in the back halls. I don't have enough Crew to do it."

"I'll get them started. Green, 16 centimeter cube?"

"That's right. And we'll just have to hope that it's not damaged."

"Jesus."

"Don't think he's been listening. I'm sure as anything that someone's been praying since this started. Not me, of course, but someone."

Gov snorted. "Go wave her in. I don't want to play this more than once."

Blagger opened the door. He looked out into the corridor. Spinner was leaning against the wall. She looked tired. "There's Stim," he said.

"I don't care what Perri says about you," she said taking the offered cup from Gov, "I still like you. A god among men."

"We'll see how you feel about me when you're on the outside of that drink."

Spinner smirked. It made her eyes crinkle on the right side of her face. "And people think you're the nice one around here."

"I'm realistic. What's your read on this?"

"I think someone's been paid to take it."

"Not a true believer?"

"No, someone who doesn't know that there's a threat. If we announce that we're missing the circuit, we might get a reaction."

"If we announce that London's on a heading right toward us, we can make sure the panic kills a few of the Sugars and we won't have to worry about evacuation," Blagger added.

Spinner punched him in the arm. "Brat. The circuit isn't connected to the murder."

"Could be our thief is just working out his frustrations or taking his last time before dying," Gov argued. Blagger sat back and watch the two. Spinner really needed to be in this office, but she'd leave the Crew the day she died and not before. *Mother, please, not today. Don't let today be the last day for this Crew.*

"I don't think so. They'd be stupid to do it this early. It was an impulsive move."

"Branch could have surprised him."

Spinner shook her head. "We'll talk about Branch later. Sun-Yi's killer is more dangerous."

"How so?" Gov raised his brows. It was a teacher's tone of voice, not a superior's. Blagger watched the movements of his head and the pulse of his heart-rate against the skin of his throat.

"He's not in control. He's sloppy." And there was nothing that annoyed Spinner more than loss of control.

Gov nodded. "True enough. We have the Crusts from the visiting area sequestered. As well as everyone who's got access to the area. Not counting the Crew, but the sensors tell me they were all in the commons at the time. We're doing interviews anyway. While they're working the docks. The sabotage. How is it connected?"

"The circuit's thief, I'd guess. Or even just someone who's been listening to the news and wants to make sure no one leaves."

"A True Believer of some stripe? I'll set Wheels on the backgrounds. Give me the list of Sugars and I'll pull them as well. The thieves? The ones you know about? So we can keep an eye on them."

"They won't steal from the Longs."

"Most people enjoy being able to walk. I'd just like to make sure that the team knows who to kneecap should they lose themselves in temptation."

"Right. This information comes from a good source, but you didn't hear it from us, right?"

"I never hear anything from you two." Gov put his

radio back on. "And I've got the recording here." He pushed a pad across the surface of his desk. Blagger sent him the requested information. Gov nodded. "You listen. I'm going to pass this on to Wheels." Wheels was a Farm's child turned computer specialist that Gov had trained when the Nurse had informed the Estate that he'd never walk. The young man was barely out of his teens, but never turned up bad information.

"Hey, is that my targeting information?" they heard him ask as the door closed behind Gov.

Spinner turned on the recording and they both leaned forward. The volume was low, but that didn't make the sound of sobbing any less heart-wrenching. "This is why I'll never do Security." She leaned against him for a moment. They watched as the Sugar-thief pulled herself together.

"Please state your name."

"Miriam Holstein," she said. She lifted her chin imperiously, but the haughty look was ruined by the red-rimmed eyes and running nose. Her lips trembled.

"Your real name."

"That is my real name." She frowned.

"And can you please identify this woman?"

"Sun-Yi Tran. My m-maid." She swallowed hard, one hand shaking as she reached out to touch the dead woman's hair.

"The truth, Ms. Holstein. We need the full truth."

"She's my best friend. My confidant. Have you ever had someone who knew all your secrets and would never betray you? That was Sun-Yi. I can't stay in here. Is there somewhere else we can go?"

"Step this way." The scene moved out of the nurse's back room into the consultation room. "And when was the last time you saw Sun-Yi?"

"She helped me fix my hair this morning before brunch. And then, she was off to work on the clothes that needed cleaning. She said she wanted to get them done before we ship out. I think she just enjoys it sometimes. She was redoing the beadwork on one of my shirts." Holstein's breath stuttered.

"Ms. Holstein, I know your reputation," Gov said quietly. "You know the Longs. We need the full truth."

"She wasn't doing anything today. At least not that she told me. And she would have. We're partners. We were partners," she corrected herself. "Oh, God, what am I going to do without her?" She hugged herself. The light glittered off of her ring. Her promise ring, if Blagger was any judge.

"Oh that poor girl," he murmured.

"She's not lying. She really doesn't know anything. Crap. I was hoping it was retaliation."

"I'd like to see if Little Miss could talk to her for us. Comfort her."

Spinner's head snapped to the side. "That's rather cold. I thought that was my purpose in life."

"She'll talk to a professional. If there was a score here, she'll talk to her." Blagger shrugged. "I don't think she's lying either. I think this was something that's confined down there, but she'll open up to someone who doesn't have a vested interest in finding a killer."

"We were, we were getting out," Holstein said quietly. "This was going to be our last Season. We were going to settle down in Amsterdam or Tirol and not worry about anything but being ourselves. No more damned parties. No more having to do my hair five different ways a day." She wiped ineffectively at her tears.

Gov leaned into her space. "Did she mention anything that was disturbing her? Did she get along with the Crusts down here?"

"She was fine. She said there was just the usual bantering and arguing that went on. They all know each other, after all. There was just the one new person working for Monestra. He had to let his last valet go. There was something about fraud or something like that."

"And what will I see if I look into Sun-Yi's background?"

"That she had two arrests when she was younger for pick-pocketing. They wanted to arrest her for... for prostitution, but she wasn't. Her parents were very particular about things like that. She went to church." Holstein smiled softly. "She tried to get me to go with her, but I couldn't make myself be a hypocrite and they'd want me to stop stealing."

"Was she worried when you saw her?" Gov was gentle and the woman obviously appreciated it. Professional courtesy, Blagger thought.

"She was just getting bored. We've got two more parties before..." she stopped. She swallowed hard. "I told you we were planning to retire."

"Could someone have found out your target?"

Holstein thought for a moment. "I suppose. I picked up a few shops this time around. And they're paying nice dividends. And we were looking to pick up a hair shop. There's a Sugar who's designing these winged things. And I think they're going to catch on next season. I'm trying to get the patent from her. It's not illegal. Just profitable. And she's new enough that she'll be an easy take."

"And you don't think anyone would kill to take that opportunity?"

"No." She shook her head. The tiny crystals threaded into her hair caught in the indirect light of the room and made flares as she moved. "I don't know why anyone would... would. Do you know, was she?"

"Yes. She was raped."

Holstein ran for the trash bin and emptied the contents of her stomach. Nurse shoved a cup of water into Gov's hand before closing the door again. Gov offered the water and Holstein rinsed her mouth. "She's never. With a man, she's never. Said that she never would."

Gov nodded his understanding. "I'll ask Nurse to give you a sedative, if you'd like."

"No, no, I'll just go back to my room."

He grimaced. "I think you'd better lie down here. There was some sort of spill up on the docks and the Crew shut down the transporters."

She laughed bitterly. "Of course. If it's one thing, it's ten."

"Ain't that the truth."

The recording moved to the seemingly endless interviews with the Crusts and Kitchens. There were flags on the important ones. Spinner skipped ahead to the first flag. After watching all the flagged interviews Blagger was willing to cram something sharp into his ears. Spinner looked more attentive. She was rewinding the recording to see something again. Blagger pulled his pad out to continue his perusal of the military's papers. There was a message for him from Little Miss. "Meet me in the orgy corner."

His lips twitched. "Give me at least an hour," he answered. The little counter in the corner of his screen was down to 19 hours and 57 minutes. His stomach bunched. "Tell me you have something."

"I think I do. Go ask Gov about Weston."

"That a Crust or Sugar?"

"Shalita refers to all the visiting Crusts by their Sugar name."

"I say again, Crust or Sugar?"

"Oh, Sugar. I need to know about the Crust, but I think the Sugar's probably interesting reading."

"Interesting. Let me pull the dossier."

Spinner put a hand on his wrist. She shook her head. "Just ask Gov."

He narrowed his eyes are her, then nodded slowly. "Right, luv." He knocked on Wheels' door.

"Come in."

Gov was leaning over the desk to look at something that Wheels had pulled up. The red-headed teenager grinned up at Blagger. "Hey, Blag."

"Hi, kiddo. Spinner wants me to ask you about Weston."

Gov's face went flat. "She pulled him too, then. I'll get him into an interrogation cell."

"You like him for it?"

"Just a hunch. Wheels is trying to find supporting evidence."

"Nothing on the tapes?"

"Oh, there's something there, but we can't see the face of the attacker."

Blagger frowned. "No, there was a camera above the door."

"There's no cameras above the door noted on our system. We've never pulled those recordings. You're sure?"

"Could be something that Kitchens uses?"

"Did you install them?"

"Not in my time here."

Gov cocked his head to the side. "Penny, sing out. Do you have a camera on 105 in the visiting crust area?"

"I hear you Gov. Let me double check. If we do, I've never found them before."

"They're mine," Lady Long's voice said quietly. The chatter on the line died almost immediately.

# CHAPTER 13

"Patch through to my system, Marsden. You have the code," Lady Long ordered. Her voice echoed a bit. She'd ducked into her alcoves for a bit of privacy. None of the guests would bother here there while she was obviously taking care of Estate business. During parties, the Estate was her responsibility. Lord Long was still glad-handing and laughing with his guests.

"Yes, Ma'am. Penny, I'll be up in a minute. Prepare to send the recordings to security. Ma'am, you'll change the code tomorrow."

"God willing."

Spinner's eyes widened. She looked at Blagger with a bit of fear in her eyes. "Ma'am, do you have eyes in the wheel-room?"

"Not yet. I'll have to get to that as soon as possible."

"I'll make a note, ma'am."

"If you need me to wire them, just let me know," Blagger stated. He didn't want to know who on his Crew had been helping without letting him in on the secret. At this point, he couldn't be sure that the Lady wasn't doing it herself. He'd never been completely sure of what her skill-set entailed. He only knew that she wasn't one to worry about past history, as long as you didn't cross her.

"Of course, Blagger." Her voice warmed slightly. "See to your Crew."

"Yes, ma'am."

He stared at Gov with eyes wider than he wanted. Gov scowled. He hadn't known about the cameras. He should have, but then, what he didn't know, he couldn't betray. A blackmail scheme of this level was incredible. He wondered if there were cameras he hadn't bothered to note in the guest rooms. Sweet mother, he wanted in on it. "Long signing off."

The chatter was light for a few minutes, and then the normal hum of words crescendoed and leveled off into the back of Blagger's mind. "Blagger, signing off." He took of his radio.

"Spinner's off."

"Gov off. Talk to Wheels if you need me." They tucked their radios away so that they didn't pick up the discussion they were going to have now. "Nothing we see in these recordings will go beyond us without explicit permission from the Lady or Marsden."

"Of course not. Only in the visiting corridors, I suppose?" Spinner's voice could have come from any of the bored Sugars upstairs.

Blagger straightened his shoulders and leaned back in his seat and angled his chin up as though he were facing a Sugar interview. Gov's lips twitched. "Amusing, both of you. But if I wanted to talk to Sugars, I wouldn't be sitting here with you. Turn it off."

"I have no idea what you're referring to, Gov. This is just our normal demeanor."

Gov snorted. "Right."

"How's Adelaide doing?" Spinner asked, relaxing.

Gov smiled, thinking about the Kitchen he was engaged to. It was a good move. Blagger approved. Normally, he had to prompt this sort of action from Spinner. She was brilliant, but never seemed to know how to interrogate people she knew. "She's well. And hopefully, she'll be moving into my quarters within the next few weeks. Granting that we still have an Estate." He lifted his brows. "Now, which thieves are we looking for?"

"We have Blensham, Lucky, Sweetbelle, Handsom, and Randy on board right now. And there are four that were identified that neither of us know."

"Let me see the list." Gov looked over the list with furrowed brows. "I'm fairly certain that Burrows is better known as Shadowboxer."

"Really?" Blagger's eyes lit up.

"Are you going to ask for his autograph?" Spinner teased.

"Man's a legend. He shook up the London Sugars for three years with his games."

"And what did he get out of his game?"

"Last I heard, he got the rights to a small Estate that's near Paris and a request that he never show his face in London Society again." Blagger shrugged. "Not the worst outcome. He's still in the Sugars Season."

"True enough. I don't recognize these other three. Are we sure of this information?"

"Yes. I trust the source implicitly. She has nothing to gain by lying."

"Why am I not surprised that there's a woman involved? Does she owe you or did you break her heart?"

"I never break hearts." Blagger smirked. "I leave people happy when I'm done. I don't know if that's how you learned to do it."

"Gov, don't get into this with him. The information is good. The source isn't going to do something to harm her source of income."

"Do you know this person?"

"No, but I know Blagger." Spinner shrugged. Gov's eyes fastened on her. "And you know he's a good judge of character."

"True."

Marsden arrived with a pad of recordings. "These must not go onto the main system."

"Got it."

He looked old. He pulled off his radio and held it behind his back. His eyes tripped over the three of them. "And when you find out who hurt her, let me know and we'll make sure he disappears from the rosters. We'll let her partner know and resolve the issue. The less the Authorities poke their pointy little noses into our business, the happier the Mistress and Master will be."

Gov nodded once. "Ask her partner if she wants to deal with this issue herself, or if she'll trust us to act in her interest."

"I will. And simply tell me when we can stop losing the feeds."

Blagger frowned. "Does the lady have eyes upstairs too?"

Marsden frowned. "She might."

"In the rooms or in the back halls?"

"There's nothing in the back halls. There is one in the transporter, but it doesn't record sound."

"Thank God," Spinner murmured. Marsden's lips quirked up.

"I wouldn't get a half-credit for you and Blagger's conversations. You're damned predictable and boring. All married couples are."

"We aren't married," they said in unison.

That gained a full smile from the older man. "Tell me when it's safe to look again."

"I will." Gov nodded. Marsden left them to review the footage. The halls were boring until they saw Sun-Yi, laughing and shaking a shirt at the woman she was walking next to. She ducked into her room, but left the door open. She was working on the beadwork and embroidery with a small smile on her face. She sang along with the music on her system. She finished the last bead and hung the shirt up. She closed the door and it remained that way until the exodus for dinner. One of the other Crusts knocked on the door. She poked her head out and flashed her hand twice — 10 minutes. She retreated and the rest of the swarm left the hallway.

Then, from room 101, out stepped a tall, thin man with a tiny mustache and straight shoulders. He knocked on her door. She opened it as she fastened the last button on her shirt. Her eyes widened. "Oh, I didn't expect it to be you."

"May I walk you up to dinner?"

"That's alright. I can find the way. You go on ahead. I still have to do my hair." She gave him a gentle, but false smile. She shut the door, or tried to. It bounced off of the wrist attached to his fisted hand. She stepped back, eyes darting from side to side.

"Mistake," Spinner murmured. Her fingers clenched into tight fists as she watched. Blagger just felt the same sick fascination violence always sparked. He wasn't a fighter. Not like Gov and Spinner. He'd have stepped back. Held his hands up in supplication and run like a bug from light if he'd seen an opening. She grabbed for the first portable thing she could.

"Leave." Sun-Yi straightened her shoulders and lifted her chin. She stared him in the eye. He lunged forward. She hit him with the perfume bottle and hit shattered. There was a little blood on his face, but that didn't stop him. He hit her twice and then dragged her from the room into the unoccupied room across the hall.

Gov changed to the next viewpoint, but Blagger couldn't watch. He stood and turned his back on the footage. He studied the pictures stuck to the office walls. There were Team pictures from the beginning of the Estate to the current group. There was Marsden as a young man, doing a rotation with Security before he was moved on to the next place. And there was Gov when he first joined the Security force, with memories of war in his eyes and a too-thin body and a pinched mouth. There was Velvet as the fresh-faced teenage gopher under Gov's arm.

There was a muffled sob from Spinner. Blagger put a hand on her shoulder, but didn't turn toward the desk. There was the entire Estate turned out to do the cleaning after the last party. And there was the birth of the Lady's last child, Borland. To the side of the pictures was the litany of the Estate. Every person who had been born or died on the Estate was featured. At the bottom of the list, in Gov's neat hand was Branch's name. Sun-Yi wasn't theirs to remember. Blagger swallowed, seeing Branch's family name instead of Long for the first time in years. Blagger would be recorded as a Long if he died. He didn't have an family to claim him – not as Blagger. Lady Long would let him remain as he was, just Blagger.

"It's done." Gov's voice was cold. "You can look now. Nothing you haven't seen."

Blagger was confronted once again with Sun-Yi's body. He shook with rage. "I just don't understand this," he said quietly. "But I'm more than willing to go find the useless, spineless creature that did this."

"I know exactly where he is."

"And I want to know who he's attached to," Spinner stated. "I want to know which Sugar is going to scream bloody murder if he disappears."

"Which Sugar is going to be forced to watch this first?" Gov asked. "He's attached to Warrenton."

"One of the thieves. If this was some sort of twisted message, I'll kill them myself," Blagger stated.

Gov put on his radio. "Sing out, Honey. Go find Mr. Warrenton and ask him to come to the office. Tell him it has to do with his ship." Gov paused. "Wheels, sing out. Does Warrenton have a ship on the docks?" He nodded. "You have the information, Honey."

"Blagger and I will…" She stopped. "I have no idea."

"Have the rest of our Stim and make sure that Warrenton doesn't get too upset. He'll think we're here for the same reason, relating to that mess on the docks. Perhaps he'll think the ships nicked each other or something." Blagger offered.

Gov considered. "No, that's fine. You two focus on the circuit. I think this is the best opportunity you have to search the last of the rooms. Keep me in the loop. Find out if some government is trying to use us."

Spinner inclined her head. "Is my make-up fine?" she asked Blagger. He turned her head gently from side to side. He nodded. As they crossed the threshold, Gov's voice stopped them.

"I'll need at least 4 hours, Blagger."

"Yes, sir," he said quietly. "You'll have it." He forced his hand to stop shaking. "And we'll do everything in our power to make sure that the decision doesn't have to be made."

"I expect nothing less."

# CHAPTER 14

"What decision?" Spinner's voice was soft.

"Evacuation. All of our thieves are clumped together on five. You'd think that the Lady had a hand in that."

She gripped his arm. "We will make sure that doesn't happen. There has to be a way to circumvent the system. Do we have the broken one?"

"No. Miserable ticks on the back of a dog make you return the broken one when you receive your new part. Have to keep strict control you know. Don't want anyone figuring out how to hack the system."

"And are we sure there's no one on the Crew who can?"

Blagger considered that as they once again headed to the upper floors. It was easier to move on the second entertaining level. There were fewer people and the ones who were there, were headed for specific support services—child care, the Nurse, or one of the connection stations. Two people who looked to be moving in a purposeful direction were ignored.

"I wouldn't say that. It's just that they could do it if there were something to hack."

"Who's on your short list?" She snuggled under his

arm, looking for the world like his girl once again.

"Mel might be able to do it. Or Mica. Wheels with someone to act as his legs and crawl under the console. You might be able to do it. Or one of the twins."

"Not you?"

"I'd already be working on it and leaving the searching to you."

Spinner nodded, to acknowledge that. She gave his arm a squeeze as the doors to the transporter closed. There was no one else in sight, which made the hallway look odd. The fifth floor looked like the rest of the floors. It was silent on the upper floors and Blogger shivered. This is what it would look like if they had to abandon the Estate. The halls would be the empty and echoing like this. There would be no one laughing in the hall. There'd be no children running through the Kitchens. The livestock would be wandering alone in their enclosure to slowly die, never knowing why the people who'd raised them suddenly disappeared.

There would be no one crying in the back hallway or making love in a ship in the back dock. There was always so much life on the Estate. It would hurt so much to see it dead—just another floating grave for the family he'd grown into. And if they couldn't make sure that everyone was out, the left behinds would be shivering in the hallways and praying to their gods, if they had any.

"Stop thinking. I can practically hear you."

"Sorry." He put his arm over her shoulders and gave them a squeeze. "If we evacuate, I expect you to look after the Crew. You understand that?"

"Why would I leave without you?" She frowned.

"Because I'll go down with the Estate. We're going to try a last ditch attempt to get out of the way of London without hitting any of the evacuation ships."

"The storm." She stopped mid-step. "You're going to put people out in the storm because it's safer than being hit? Are you insane?"

"Out of the Estate and straight down. Hit ground and put up any shielding you have and hope for the best. The Estate, we're going to send straight forward on its heading and hope to all the stars that we won't run into the Baldwin or the Ameris."

"And even if you do, there's few to die there." She swallowed. "Thieves," she stated. "Where are we heading?"

"14, 25, 19, 39, and 54."

"You're getting closer. Too tired to mess with my head?" She raised her brows.

"Not enough differences to make it interesting. If you're not having to run up and down the floors, what's the point of annoying you?"

"I really hope that your insanity isn't catching."

"You'd have it already. Oh, wait, you're Crew. You're infected. It's too late, I'm afraid to say. It'll just grow."

She took his keycard from his pocket and opened the first room. "This is?"

"Lorton. That's the traveling name. If it's someone else, I won't know without seeing him."

Lorton's room was neater than a military barracks. "Traveling with a Crust?"

"No. His valet stayed at the Ballard Estate. Finally asked his lover to marry him."

"Where do you hear these things?"

"Ballard head of Crew was calling to fix our position before the Season moved on. We tend to pass on information that might affect things. The Estate provides Crust support to Sugars traveling without if they request it. Marsden probably gets a formal list, but I get to hear the why's which are always more important."

"Gossip."

"Always." He gave her his second best sweet smile and turned into the closet. He found a stack of datapads. He raised his brows and set to reviewing them. He laughed out loud. "This one isn't our bird," he stated.

"How can you tell?"

"There's no profit in getting caught with all this. He's going to need a trip to a City and there's no way he'd let himself get caught up in a place like this. He's probably twitching and trying to figure out how to get his loot to the room without anyone noticing that they're a bit lighter than they were."

"He's pick-pocketing at Season events? What sort of idiot does that?"

"A fairly successful one. At least on the picking part of it. I don't know if the finances are real or if he's traveling on a loan and a prayer."

"You ever tried that? I always paid ahead."

"I've travelled on a smile." He reviewed the pads for anything usable anyway. "Dear heart, did you know that Miles Penderson is dating Julianne Madras?"

"Who are they and why would I care?"

Blagger laughed out loud. "Miles Penderson is the heir to the Manchester Estate. And Madras is the daughter of one of the Amsterdam owning families. Both of them are also supposed to be engaged to someone else."

"Good for them. They should follow their hearts."

"Romantic, but not practical."

"Why should this be anything I need to worry about?" He didn't call her on the minute twitch around her left eye that meant she was lying to him. He didn't want her to get rid of any of her tells.

"You don't. No bearing on anything you do. If you cared about the outside world, then maybe, it'd affect you more." He continued to peruse the gossipy emails and the private calendars of the Sugars that Lorton had picked up. He set them back where he'd found them. He paused. "Unless he's actually a blackmailer and I've read it wrong."

Spinner didn't respond immediately. "I don't think he is," she said. Her voice was subdued. He went to see what she'd found. There, in the traveling box under his bed was his Authority badge and weapon.

Blagger bit his lip to keep from cursing.

"We're fucked."

His head snapped towards her. "I don't know that. Let's be sure it's real before we panic."

"It's real. Look at those scratches. You don't get those without wearing the damnedable things."

"Something I should know?"

"I might possibly have known a Nob a bit better than expected."

"Ain't we all." Blagger considered his "uncle" who'd kept him fed on Saturdays, while he pumped him for information on the Sugars and the Spice.

"My brother," she said quietly. "It killed him in the end. The injustice. The power plays. The money that really decided things. It ate him up from the inside out and there was nothing that we could do to save him."

"How old were you?" he asked softly.

"He stepped off a dock when I was eleven. Mother never recovered." Her voice was a whisper.

Blagger let it go. If they survived, he'd see about purging her grief. "See if there's any indication of what he's looking for, or if he's left the service."

She brightened. "I'd forgotten about that. He could be retired on his takings."

"A few rewards and a bit of dosh here and there to forget? Little Miss is sure he's a thief."

"And how sure would she have to be to identify him to us?"

"Not much. But we can find out. We'll ask Wheels to look at the number."

"Won't that attract attention we don't want right now?"

"Not if he's half the hacker Gov's taught him to be." Blagger dropped a quick note to Wheels through the internal system. He didn't want to sing this information out. It was sure to panic the more than a few former Spice membership in the Estate. Lady Long herself might take interest. She didn't need any more worries right now. "And if he is a Nob still, do we bring him in? Get him on our side?"

"Not until we've decided what to do with Sun-Yi's killer."

"Until we can claim he ran off you mean?"

"Yes, that. Can we create a false trail for a ship? Something that could go walk-about without us noticing?"

"A hopper that picked him up? Not until the storm clears." Blagger grimaced. "Let's hope Little Miss was right about him. Plenty of Nobs who ain't."

"Your accent is slipping."

"Right. Sugar," he sighed. "I'm going to head back to his boring, brown clothing again. Couldn't the man at least have a bit of color in his wardrobe?"

"That's better." She flashed him a quick smile. Her sadness was forgotten again.

The suits were all the same. The shirts did have a bit of difference to them in weave and material. There were waistcoats in the very back that were soft pastels with the shine of silk. There was no indication that there were any weapons on him. There was no indication that he carried the badge with him either. No damage to any of the linings or the pockets. He had two pairs of shoes there – one formal, one informal. They held the scuffs of repeated wearings. He would be a forgettable face in the crowd. It was a brilliant idea. Blagger couldn't pull it off, but someone like Gov might. His ties matched his waistcoats. The one thing his jackets did have were deep pockets.

"I think he's retired."

"I've got his fix-it kit. He's got nothing we can use."

Blagger frowned. "Is there a false bottom in that one?"

Spinner cocked her head to look at the side. "It might." He went to investigate the desk while she tapped on the bottom to see if it would pop. "I think it's an electric lock. Let me have your pad."

He handed it over and there was a quiet moment while she set the electronic pick to cycling. A panel in the bottom popped open. She lifted the false bottom out and stared down. Her face went red. "Blag."

He went to rescue her from the evils of naughty pictures. There was only one thing that could have created that shade of red on her cheeks. He stared down and whistled. "I sure hope those are real." He made copies of all of the pictures with his pad and saved them out to the shared file that was maintained in strictest confidence in a sub-sub-sub folder that was password protected. Spinner thumped his arm. "What?"

"See what's under it." He shifted the prints out of the way and found himself confronted with a small leather-bound book. He opened it to find it was in code. He frowned and scanned it in. He let his program work in the background while he flipped through it. "Addresses?"

"Accounts I think. Blackmailer gets another check." They set the room to rights and slipped on to the next. Which was actually the next highest number on Spinner's insistence. "Bludgren."

Spinner stared at the picture on the side-table. "Is this who I think it is?" She pointed at the half-naked woman looking over her shoulder with a fall of hair obscuring all but one eye.

"Yes." Blagger swallowed. "That is, I, well, there's no reason why she wouldn't be in a picture here. He's one of her patrons, yeah?"

"Are there pictures of you like this running around?"

"No one keeps my picture."

"I would."

"The one of us in the commons doesn't work for you."

"You mean the one that has both of us in full kits and covered from head to toe in grit and oil because of the external dock door malfunction?" She raised a brow to punctuate the statement.

"That's the one. Mystery being an aphrodisiac and all."

"That isn't mystery. Besides, I was thinking something that actually showed your face. Or are you that wanted?"

"No comment?"

She shook her head. "I'm not even going to ask. I'll take the bed storage. You get the closet. You get the next one, since this is the third on your list." She added when he opened his mouth to complain.

"That's devious. You just don't like clothing."

"I wear it. I just don't know enough about it to make the best judgments." Her smile was as fake as an Audrey Press painting. He stuck his tongue out at her and went to the closet.

"Liar," he called over his shoulder. Bludgren's closet was bursting with color, like the plumage on a tropical bird. The first set of papers had his base in Dusselburg. The next one was Frankfurt. The last was Berlin. He shook his head. He'd never been to any of the Cities, but he was sure that they weren't full of men dressed like this. Mother of sangria, there were even feathers and spangles on this jackets and vest. "This is… I can't believe a tailor even made these." He poked at one of the vests and his finger bounced off. He opened it and stroked along the inside lining. "Either he's storing some sort of tech in here or it's bullet-proofed," he called. The feathers made more sense now. They'd distract from the distressingly utilitarian armor underneath. He tapped at it. It wasn't thick enough to be the circuit, but he desperately wanted to cut open the lining to see what it was instead.

"I think he has enough people after him to make that reasonable." Spinner's voice was light. "The names here all have hits on them."

"And where did you learn that, luv?"

"You gossip with your friends, I gossip with mine."

"You're going to lose your reputation as the sweet one at this rate." Blagger continued through the closet. There were shoes in simple black that were covered in black glitter. He tried to wipe the glitter off of his hands. All he got for his trouble was glittering pants.

"Someone thinks I'm sweet? Why? Because I put up with you for increasingly long periods of time? Or is it the hair? I've been thinking of chopping it off."

"Don't you dare. It's short enough already."

"What on earth was he doing that go him this many enemies?"

"You haven't seen his closet. I think it's possibly that he's upset the fashion police enough that they're making sure he's not a problem anymore. Sister spangles, this is dreadful. Watch, it'll be all the rage next Season." Blagger found a box in the far back corner that looked like a bed storage box. He unlocked it and found a wealth of papers. His eyes widened. "Spin, come here."

"What?" She looked over his shoulder. Her fingers tightened into a death grip. "Are those what I think they are?"

"The foundation documents that went wandering a few years ago? Why yes, they are. The question is, what are we going to do about it?"

"It doesn't look like a circuit or an admission of guilt about a murder. I say we close the box, replace it very carefully and remember to duck all the weapons that will be flung at this..." she drifted off. When Blagger looked up, she was staring in horror at the feathered vests. "What is he? Part bird?"

"I think he's playing the part of a fashion designer. Or something equally out there."

"Like the girl in the silver lame?"

"Let us not discuss that outfit. It offends my eyes."

"And these spangles aren't giving you hives yet?"

"I have glitter all over my pants. It's as much thought about his dressing that I care to make." He traced the air just above the documents. He didn't want to touch them and risk damaging them. "How much do you think he'll make in ransom for those?"

"I think he'll manage to escape with his life without having to turn on his partners."

"True. I was thinking he might buy himself a lordship somewhere."

"Depends on his ability to outlive whomever helped him with this insanity. Just close it. We don't want to be too close to them. I don't know about you, but I don't want any trace of me on them."

"True enough." He closed the box and set it back where it came from. "I'm sure he'll know we looked."

"But he'll hopefully be smart enough to keep his mouth shut about it without any sort of persuasion."

Blagger nodded. The foundation documents were from the Geneva archives. The archive contained the documents that set out the inter-city agreements, the contract negotiations that had established the very Estate that they now lived on, and the history of the world. Fourteen documents had walked out of the archive without an alarm being set off. It had taken the Authorities over six months to discover the full extent of the heist. Just being this close to them made his fingers itch. It was an incredible feeling to be near something that important.

He followed Spinner into the main room. The desk didn't turn up anything to catch his attention beyond the fact that he had a meeting with Little Miss set up for the next night. Hopefully they'd both survive long enough to have it. Spinner made a little note of triumph as she got the last box to open. "Oh," she said.

"What?" He turned in his chair.

"Do you think he'd miss one little one?" The diamonds and spinel glittered in the light. "I mean, there's got to be thousands in here. He won't miss just a little one."

Blagger found his magnifier. He briefly considered getting an implant when this was finished, but dismissed it. He didn't need any augmentation yet. He put lifted one of the jewels to look for the registration marks around the rim. His brows rose. There was no mark, but he would be willing to put his life on the fact that they were real. "These are old and real. There's no registration of them."

"Strict currency then." Spinner lifted up a 4mm white diamond. She dropped it into her cleavage. She waved a hand over the box.

"No, I promised the Lady I was over that sort of behavior."

"He's a thief, not a Sugar. I don't think he falls under the proscription."

Blagger frowned as he thought. *He was in the Nurse's office, laying on the recovery bed after the tests they'd run to reassure themselves that he wasn't going to die on them. Lady Long had taken his hand. "I've seen your record and I don't care," she told him bluntly. "I need your promise that you will not steal from any target that will harm the Estate."* He looked down at the jewels.

He shook his head. He closed the box. "This idiot could do a lot of damage to us with this sort of cash behind him. Even if he is on the short-list for stupid actions that will soon get him killed."

Spinner sighed. She didn't return the jewel and there was no way he'd ever ask her to. He didn't know what promises she'd made, but he did know that she didn't come to them with the same history he had or the amount of medical help he'd needed. Whatever agreements she had with the mistress of the estate was between the two of them. The box went back under the bed and they made their way to the next room.

# CHAPTER 15

"Cranston. Traveling with two Crusts."

"You're keeping notes on who needs to be searched down there, right?"

"Yes."

Spinner rubbed her eyes.

"Do you need Stim?" he asked.

"No, I'm good for awhile more."

He opened the door and bowed her in. She laughed as she passed him, with an inclination of her head. Her shoulders were straighter now and he called it good. She stepped into the closet. He headed for the storage area and stopped in the middle of what looked like a house after the Authorities were finished with it. "Sweet lady of Mercy, if I ever end up leaving a room like this, do me a favor and shoot me in the head."

"Do you think someone got here before us or is she just a slob?"

"I think her Crusts need an instruction manual on how to do their job. There's no way that this place should be as messy as this." Blagger toed his way to the bed. The covers were splayed across the floor. He looked under the pillows first and there was a datapad with nothing of use on it. The knife strapped to the headboard was sharp enough, but it was in a very bad position to pull quickly if you were lying down. He cocked his head to the side to figure out why the hilt was angled toward the top. It only made sense if you were standing up. Why on the bed though? He shook his head.

He found the storage boxes unlocked. "I do not like this," he murmured. "Spin, someone beat us to this place and they were not neat."

"They tossed the closet too." Spinner's voice was disgusted. "I can't figure out if they bothered to take anything or if they were just being cruel."

He knelt down by the box. There was a mass of wires and resistors laying on top of a jumble of tools. Given that it was a mess anyway, he poked through it looking for anything of use. There was no flicker of green. He frowned. Why was he so sure that the Helion was here? Perhaps because it was so badly tossed. None of the boxes turned up anything. He checked the system for special actions and found only a few quick liaisons.

"She's trying to blend in, that's all I can tell from this mass of fabric. She must have taken something important."

"Or thrown over a lover. I haven't seen a tantrum like this since Marsden's wife left him."

"Marsden's wife left him? How did I not hear about this?" Spinner stuck her head out of the closet.

"It was about three months before you came. She left him. Left the Estate with a Sugar. She became his Crust."

"What did she do here?"

"She worked on the Farms, I think. She left Penny with Marsden. It worked out for us, but he was not well for awhile. And he tore up the rooms pretty badly. Penny was, oh, three or four, I think." Blagger shrugged. "I just kept handing him the drinks until he passed out and when he woke up he felt much better. Well, at least he couldn't think beyond getting to the nurse to get something for his head."

"So, you think this is something similar? That our thief here got turned over and did this to her own things?"

"I'm not sure. Could be a Crust that did it. If they were in a relationship and something went wrong. Or, hell, if they're supposed to be partners and Cranston is treating them like actual servants." He sorted through the next box. "I had a thought."

"That's unusual."

"Our thief might still be carrying the circuit. Or it may be on the entertaining floors."

"Please don't say things like that. You'll make me cry."

His head snapped up at that. "Don't scare me like that!"

Spinner's laughter echoed in the closet like a mad scientist. "You're too easy."

"I've gotten used to all these honest people."

"You mean Mel?"

"Well, Mel. And Shalita. And Nurse. Well, maybe Nurse."

"Not Marsden?"

"In this Estate? Are you insane?" He paused. "Well, you are, but that's neither here nor there."

"Now, this is neat." She came out carrying a shoulder bag. "Look at how it's strapped. It can rest on your stomach and hide under your clothing. Or even down your skirt. There's so many options."

"You'd like one?"

"Yes."

"I'll see what I can do for you birthday. Or our anniversary."

She looked up. "We have an anniversary?"

"Of when you moved into my room."

"Oh, that. That would be nice. Are you expecting me to get something?"

"No, that would break my sanity."

She put the bag away after searching every pocket. Then, she headed for the desk. "If I had to guess, I'd say that every piece of her clothing is on the floor. Does she have jewelry?"

Blagger gestured around the room. Cranston's jewelry glittered in the soft lighting like stars in an old-fashioned video. "I think there's some."

Spinner rolled her eyes at him. She turned her attention to the desk and he returned to his search. "This is useless. The system's been disconnected."

"Paranoid then?"

"It's possible. But looking at the room, it's for good reason. Who is our next suspect?"

"Holstein." The room was a relief. Everything was neatly stowed. They had to be more careful, but there was less chance of simply missing something. "I get the storage again, right?"

Spinner considered, tapping a finger on her lips. The berry stain had faded. If they were going to go among the Sugars again, she'd need to redo it. His shirt was starting to pull free of his trousers. "Yes." There was a box of supplies for Holstein's ship. Blagger paused when he found the picture of Sun-Yi and Holstein smiling and waving their matching rings.

"This is Sun-Yi's wife," he reminded Spinner.

"They're actually married? I assumed they were simply partners." Spinner grimaced. "I should have thought. Most people actually do go through with things like that. And she did have the ring on. Somehow that makes it worse."

"I feel strange about this one. On the one hand, she is a thief and we do need to search, on the other, she's grieving. And I don't like her for the robbery."

Spinner sighed. "We don't have a choice. The search has to be done. Personal feelings have nothing to do with it."

"Don't they? I don't kid myself. I know that I won't be a thorough with her as I would be with Weston. I'd be looking for other things to torture Weston over. I don't think Holstein needs the same level of interrogation."

"But will it be thorough enough to find the part if it's here?" Spinner raised a brow and crossed her arms over her chest.

"Of course. I'm still a professional. Well, not any longer, usually, but I've got my pride."

"Then search."

Her storage boxes turned up nothing spectacular, except a wealth of jewelry and small data devices. Petty thievery on top of the grand plans and cons, but who didn't indulge? He rolled one of the rings around in his hand, then put it back where he'd found it. He looked under the pillows and discovered a knife. That didn't faze him. Any thief that didn't carry protection was an idiot. It was too bad that Sun-Yi hadn't had one too.

His throat tightened. He might not be married to Spinner, but the thought of something happening to her, he stopped the thought. If something happened to Spinner, he would already be dead. Thinking protective thoughts about her was bound to get him into trouble. And anyone that could take her would have already eliminated him. He'd either have been a hostage or a soft target.

He plumped the pillow and put it back. He opened the small box next to the chair. He made an involuntary sound of joy. There was an extra data connection there. He transferred the data to his pad for future perusal. "Did you find something nice?"

"Just some data to parse. Anything in her closet I need to worry about?"

"Not yet. I think she's carrying a gun of some sort. I've found holsters sew into the linings."

"Knife holster too?"

"Not yet. Just gun. I think," she paused. "Aha! Here, in her boot. She can keep a knife at her ankle."

He read through the next few documents that the program had translated. His gorge rose. "'Collateral damage' and 'fray adjacent losses'. Emotionally dead reanimated corpses of bloated warthogs."

"Have you ever seen a warthog?"

"I watch educational programming," he answered swiftly. "And they suit. These sons of a pestilent rat are talking about killing thousands just to make a point about some treaty that reduces tariffs. As though they think that justifies sacrificing real, true human beings. That cutting short the life of some innocent child is okay, just to make money. I cannot understand it. I will not conscience it. And I will not be party to some mindless drone's idea of what a war should be."

"What are you going to do?"

"I'm going to leak the memos from both sides."

"Can you do that without getting killed or bringing it back on the estate?"

"Yes. And I'm not going to do anything about it until we find the thrice-buggered circuit."

"Three times a night? Does that take drugs?"

He gave her a half-smile. "If I thought you actually cared about the answer, I'd give you a lecture on refractory periods. As you don't, let me say, no, it doesn't. So long as you're young, male, and horny. And you can take turns."

Spinner's brows furled. "I think I need diagrams," she said finally. "But I really don't want to know, do I?"

"No, luv. You don't want to know. Sufficient to say, I'll be posting this either as a last-ditch as the Estate goes down, or from a secure location. London doesn't deserve my loyalty after this stunt. And Lancaster can go whistle."

"You think our London military man is behind this?"

Blagger sighed. "If only it were that simple. No, I think he's a fray adjacent casualty himself."

"You think it's a professional thief. Or a professional anarchist, not a true believer?"

He grimaced. "If the smog storm hadn't come up so quickly, I think our thief would be off this ship. I know I would be. Simply grab a hopper and head to one of the Cities. Sell the circuit to someone in the black and move on. If they ever trace it, who's to say who took it? The buyer can't say. The thief won't say. And no government in the System will admit to anything about it."

"The last one is Shadowboxer?"

"That's what Gov believes. I'm willing to give him the benefit of the doubt. On to Burrows." Blagger felt the smile on his face. "Did you hear about the volcano?"

Spinner tucked herself against his side. "No? What did he do?"

"He convinced an entire group of people that he could control it. And that he'd set it off, killing their village."

"Where was this? Someone living on real ground?"

"Yes. There's a group of people who are so rich, they have actual ground that's not been destroyed yet. That being the case, the one thing they fear above all else is?"

"Their ground being destroyed. But no one controls volcanoes."

"Doesn't matter. Only matters that people believe it can be done. Maybe they thought he was like a cloud artist, only working in lava. I don't rightly know. But I do know that he ended up with a rumored take of one million credits from each of the affected parties."

"Rumors from whom? Who would admit to something like that?"

Blagger smiled. "He's just the most famous thief. If Burrows actually is Shadowboxer, he's the top of the crowd. He's the thief that thieves claim to have been tutored by. It's said he doesn't even hide his tattoos when he's around the Sugars. They accept him completely. They even say that he charmed the governments of Washington, Paris, and Maylay into giving him papers claiming that he works for them. Can you imagine? He's got diplomatic immunity for stealing."

Spinner laughed. "Fairy stories for good little thieves."

Blagger scowled at her. "He's real and the stories are real. I've got evidence and I'll show it to you someday. When we get out of this. I've been clipping stories about him forever."

"And the immunity?" She opened the door. He grabbed her wrist before she broke the alarm beam.

"I'm not positive. I haven't had a chance to wander around the Washington servers before." He re-routed the alarm system. He had to wonder what he'd missed though. If there was one alarm, there was sure to be more. "Do be careful when you're searching. I don't know how paranoid he is these days." He strolled into the closet. There was no way that he wasn't going to take the chance to model himself after the Shadowboxer.

His suits were exquisitely tailored in soft dove greys and melting chocolates. His vests and ties were pure silk. And his shirts were actual cotton. His shoes were old-fashioned. A statement perhaps. Or perhaps practicality where the suits were indulgence. He searched each coat for papers. He found three passports, two full wallets with different names, and four sets of picks that were carefully hidden in pockets built into the backs of his coat.

The box on the floor called to him and he opened it slowly. He'd read stories about booby-trapped boxes that could sting you if you were impatient. He sifted through the piles of albums. It seemed he wasn't the only person who kept copies of the news articles about The Shadowboxer. He scanned through the familiar pages until he found the hand-written notes next to them. He devoured those little critiques and corrections. The safest way in their connected world to keep something private was to write it down in hard-copy. It wasn't inexpensive by any stretch of the imagination, but it was still effective.

He replaced the albums one by one when he didn't find a hidden drawer or false bottom in the box. "Blagger, come here. What is this?"

Spinner held up a vaguely familiar tool. Blagger stared at it for a long moment, sorting through memories. He'd only ever seen it once. When he was much younger. One of his "uncles" had one. "Uncle William said that it was the only way to open City level consoles. You use the end to pop open the panels. If you don't have one you have to either cut the panels open or you have to get an electronic key like the government workers use."

"Does it work on all consoles?"

A very sick ball settled in Blagger's stomach. "Yes." He swallowed hard. Mother of mercy, please no, he thought.

"And what sort of traces does it leave?"

"If you use it properly? None."

Spinner looked up at him. "I think we need to search every inch."

Blagger shook his head. "It'll be in the bed."

"What?"

"Most expensive thing he's stolen on this trip. He'll keep it close."

"In the bed?"

"Tell me you won't kiss it if you see it sitting there."

"Unlike you, I do not have an unhealthy relationship with the Estate." She sniffed. Then, she seemed to see something in his face. "Oh, Kali. I'm sorry. I'm so sorry. If it ends up being true. I am so sorry."

"Don't be. He's a thief. That's what I love about him. But doing this? This crosses the line. I'm three steps from sending out a mass announcement into the ballroom saying 'if you happen to see a bright green box, please report it to a member of the Estate staff.' Only people in the know might panic. Everyone else will think it's some sort of scavenger hunt." He rolled his eyes. He pulled back the covers and ran a hand along the plush mattress. He stopped at the hard edge. He closed his eyes. "I still want his autograph," he murmured.

"I'm sure Gov will let you do some of the interrogation." She patted his thigh. "Who else would he brag to, but his greatest fan?"

"Right." He pulled the sixteen by sixteen box out from under the mattress. It was as offensively green as he'd always remembered. And it seemed to be intact.

"Oh, thank all the stars in heaven," Spinner breathed. She reached for it. Then, she paused, frowning. "That isn't ours is it?"

"No, it's not." Blagger turned the unit over in his hands. "And it's too small to be London's." Their eyes met. "But we should be able to make it work. I'll call Penny."

"I'll keep looking. How large would the one in London be?"

"Something around a meter square, I believe. I'll get the dimensions. We have to check his ship now, just to see if there's any others."

"And his Crust?"

"I don't think we need to worry about him. We're going to be rifling through all of his things anyway to make it look like he bolted."

Spinner turned back from her search to stare at him. "Oh, him," she said finally. "At least I'm not worried about his master bitching about his disappearance."

"No, I don't think it'll be an issue." Blagger put on his radio.

"And furthermore," Marsden's voice chided, "I do not believe that there is any gain in panicking the guests."

"Marsden, Gov, sing out."

"I hear you, Blagger."

"Gov, here."

"I need a team to 554. Mica, sing out."

"Mica, here."

"Grab Trenton and meet me in the back hall of the fifth guest floor."

"On the way, Boss."

"Tell me that's good news," Marsden prompted.

"It's tempered news. No evacuation."

"Thank God." Gov exhaled heavily.

"But I think there's another Estate that's in the same situation."

"A back-up plan."

"Yes."

"I'll make some calls."

"Honey, here. Blagger, sing out."

"Blagger hears you." Spinner found a second green cube and held it close to her body as she continued to look. Her eyes lit up as she found a delicate necklace attached to the underside of the bed. A key dangled from the chain. She raised her brows.

"Who am I looking for?"

"Burrows. Ask him to join you in a secure location. Tell him it's something to do with his ship."

"Acknowledged. I'll let him think it's about the issue on the docks."

"Remind me to buy you a drink sometime."

Honey laughed. The sound of it made him smile. He felt the giddiness of relief wash through his body. They were going to live. "I'll meet Mica, you talk to Gov?" Spinner rocked the Helion in her arms like a baby.

"Oh, I don't think so. You can talk to Gov."

"You can both talk to me," Gov stated in Blagger's ear.

"I have to get the work started in the wheelhouse."

"Tell the princess to put her radio in," Marsden ordered.

"Spinner, link up."

She rolled her eyes. "Spinner here."

"Be alert, we have guests missing."

"What else can go wrong?" she groused. Blagger glared at her. She stuck her tongue out at him. "Do we have anyone incoming near 554?"

"We have five guests we can't find in the main entertaining areas." Marsden said. "Wheels is helping us search the cameras."

"Here's hoping it's an orgy somewhere," Blagger muttered.

Marsden snorted. "Your life was far too interesting for your age. Feel free not to share."

"Come on, you know you love it."

Spinner tapped her teeth. "I don't know if we're in any

shape to continue passing down in the Sugar area."

"No, they're all starting to ravel and sag. They just haven't been causing trouble because everyone knows that something happening on the docks could be deadly. We'll need to let them free soon though. Before they start getting into more trouble."

"I have one more place to go."

Gov entered the room. "In a few minutes." He gestured for Rolls to move forward and start recording. "There's more than one thing painted that color?"

"Have your people seen something in this color that's about the size of a hassock?" Spinner asked. She got to her feet easily.

"There's something like it in the kid's center, but it's soft," Rolls offered. "But maybe down with the farms?"

"Mel, sing out." Spinner said suddenly.

"Mel, here."

"The Burrows ship. Has it been fixed?"

"Not yet. It's closest to the door and we're only about half-way through." The young woman sounded drained. Blagger longed to give her a hug and a pinch on the cheek to keep her going. There was no time though.

"Don't fix it in the first run. Have Metro search it. We're looking for Helions."

"Got it." Her voice was stronger now. "Anything else?"

"Not right now."

"What have you got for me?"

"Two Helions," Spinner offered. "And a key for his ship. And a lot of things to search?" She gave Gov a sweet smile.

Rolls snickered. His hair was still close cropped to his skull. He was just off of his military service. "Want to tell me what I'm looking at?"

"This is a Helion circuit that isn't ours," Blagger said holding it up. "It's got a registry number here. Can the camera get a clear scan of it?"

"I've got it."

"And this one is ours," Spinner held up the circuit. "See the registry mark and the picture of the duck on the top?"

"Why is there a duck on it?"

"Because Drake put it in?" Blagger said. Drake had been the head of the Crew before Blagger had arrived. He drew his symbol on all of the expensive things he put in. It was his promise that it was done properly and his offer to take the blame if something went wrong with it. He'd died in his sleep five years ago.

Rolls raised his brows. "Why a duck?"

"Drake is a duck." Spinner raised her brows to mirror his look.

"Must have been hard to hold a screwdriver with wings." Rolls tapped his lip as though he were thinking deeply. Spinner punched him in the arm. Rolls laughed. "I am very glad that I have this moment on camera."

"Why's that?" Gov looked up from the desk he was searching.

"Because no one will believe that I caught out Spinner. Hell, I don't believe I did it and I was here."

"I'm tired."

"It was a sound tactical decision."

"Gov, I'm going to take the Helion to Mica," Blagger said.

"No, let Spinner go. I need your expertise on these files."

"Spinner's perfectly capable of answering your questions."

"Blagger."

"Right. Tell Mica I expect this to be done and ready for testing soonest. And start sending out the distress call and let the Penderson Estate that we're heading in their direction."

Spinner clicked through the math for a moment. "Straight back and to the right then?"

"You know the layout."

She grimaced. She nodded. "I'll be back. Eventually. Or

I'll meet you in Security." The door closed behind her.

Gov tapped the desk with one fingernail. "How many Estates are in our way?"

"Since we can't see where anyone's drifted due to electrical interference in the storm? Since the cameras are effectively blind? And we've got every window sealed up tight? Who knows? Before we were blinded? There were three Estates close enough to be in trouble if we drifted too far. Penderson was straight behind us. We should be able to angle around the Wilson which is that way. Baldwin and Ameris were retethering before the storm. And London's in that direction. And, if I'm remembering correctly, up there is the Wandering Sands."

"And we're going to be flying blind?"

"In an attempt to get out of the way of London when they cut our tether. We just have to hope that no one's moved too far. I need to talk to the Wilson and see if they've gotten the message from London and moved."

"Does it have to be you?"

Blagger looked at Gov in confusion. "Well, I suppose Spinner could call. Most people know she's a navigator."

"I want you to talk to Burrows."

His brown eyes opened wide. He blinked. "You want me to do the interrogation?"

"No, I just want you to chat with him." Gov smirked. "And if that chat happens to be happening on camera and happens to give us a full confession all the better."

"I'm not in Security. The only reason we ran the whole search is well,"

"Because trying to stop Spinner is like trying to harness a smog-storm?"

"I was going to say, because we knew what we were looking for." Blagger's arms tightened on the circuit. "But we need to find out who this one belongs too."

"The registry will tell us that. I'll have Wheels look it up. It's not like we have the ability to get it back to them right now, is it?"

"No, the storm's going to be blowing for at least another two days."

Gov nodded. "When Honey gets him into a private room, with a bit of food and drink, I want you to talk to Burrows. Ask him about his famous heists. Ask him about his tattoos. Ask him where he got his ship, just keep him talking."

"But maybe ask him to brag about stealing Helions and things, too?" Blagger closed his eyes to let the bitterness go. "Ask him to sign my scrapbook. Things like that, eh?"

"Things like that. Works out well for both of us."

"Let me walk Rolls through our search."

----------

Spinner settled on the floor of the wheelhouse. She opened the panel and shut off the power. She took a breath to steady her hands and focus her mind. Installing the Helion could be as delicate as removing it, especially if there was damage they hadn't noticed first time out. She grounded the unit, then lined up each wire in succession. She tightened the tiny screws. Then, she turned the power on to the panel. Green lights lit across the top of the panel and a small orange light started to glow on the Helion.

"Helion alarm resolved," Penny said.

"Thank whoever is listening," Marsden murmured. "Good work, Crew. I'll have the kitchens send down something sweet."

"You are a prince among men," Mica purred. She had a crush on the butler, but he didn't seem to notice it. Maybe that was the project to set Blagger on next. "Make sure it's got chocolate or there'll be no hot water."

"Mercenaries. All of you are mercenaries. I blame the princess."

"Since I'm the one who put the damned thing back in, I want the largest piece."

# CHAPTER 16

Honey leaned against the wall outside of the private interview room. Her eyes were closed, lashes dark and her eye make-up glittering. Velvet was sitting on the desk across from the door. He had his stun-gun out and was making a convincing case that he was awake with wide eyes. His hand didn't shake from too much the Stim that probably made up the majority of his bloodstream. "Hey, Blagger. Honey was sure you'd be here."

"Evidence delivery to be locked up." He offered the Helion that was from some other estate. He pitied the crew there. They'd have to deal with the Authorities to get it back. "And Gov promised I could get his autograph."

Honey laughed at that, her voice rough with half-sleep. "We're actually all going to survive this right?"

"Mother willing."

"Oh, good. I'll have to take up praying or something. Where's your better half?"

"She's programming the blind run or tending to, um, more delicate feminine concerns."

"Great timing," Honey snorted. "I swear, our bodies try their best to destroy us. Though there's nothing better for cramps than a little closeness." She smirked as Velvet blanched at the thought. Blagger patted his head.

"Don't worry. She'll only make you do it if you're weak enough to promise her anything she wants."

Velvet frowned. "Well, I do sort of miss having someone else to take the pressure off. Are you sure that we can't convince you to start joining us again?"

"Not on a regular basis. But I'll allow the option."

"That's all we can ask. Now, get out of my line of fire, or go in and see him already."

"I'm working up my nerve, ain't I?" Blagger could feel his accent shifting. He looked down at his clothes. He quirked a half-smile at the two security officers. "Well, this is gonna be odd." He straightened his shirt and tried to brush the glitter off of his pants. He only ended up with it on his hands. Velvet's lips twitched and Blagger cocked his head to the side. "What?"

"You've got glitter right here." The security officer reached out and brushed at a cheekbone with his thumb. It didn't help and they both knew it wouldn't.

"Flirt." Blagger shifted on his feet.

"Go."

"Right." He lifted a hand to the door and it opened easily. "Hello, Mr. Burrows." He offered the man a friendly smile, but didn't offer him his hand. Burrows was easily three inches taller than Blagger, with patches of pure white at his temples. His face was creased with smile lines. The corners of his eyes crinkled up with some unknown joke. His clothes were carelessly high quality. His tie was loose now and the top button undone. His sleeves were rolled up and revealed a delicate tattoo running up and around his arm.

He had a gold pocket-watch on his vest and a revolving digital photograph of a woman's foot, hand, and eyes on his lapel. Blagger wasn't sure if it were all the same woman or if it meant he had three lovers. He'd have to ask around, so as not to make mistakes the next time he was in Society. He set his pad down on the table and settled himself in the

other metal chair. The chairs were both bolted down,
along with the table. The room was covered by several
cameras. One of which was broadcasting just outside the
room, so that Velvet and Honey could watch.

"And you are?" Burrows prompted.

"Blagger Long. I'm the head of the Pit Crew. There's
been a disturbance at the docks and I'm afraid your ship
was damaged." He grimaced. He pulled up the video feed
from Metro's camera to show him the sabotage.

Burrows didn't blink or react with any sort of surprise.
"And you're pulling all the owners in to discuss these
things?"

"We're working to repair the ships and hopefully no
one will be the wiser. The parts seem to still be there, but
we won't be sure until the work is finished."

Burrows' brow knit down into a furious frown. He
leaned forward and his eyes narrowed. "Take off your
shirt."

Blagger blinked. "Mr. Burrows."

The thief smiled. "Please?" He turned his wrist and
Blagger's eyes ran over the design there. He leaned forward
a bit, then raised his brows.

"Oh. Right. Ain't going to stand on ceremony?"

"Or demand proper language."

"Sweet mother of mercy," Blagger breathed as his eyes
continued to run up the tattoo until it disappeared under
the crisply folded blue sleeve. He loosened his own tie and
pushed back his right sleeve. Burrows studied the revealed
design. His smile widened.

"Well done, that."

"Thank you, sir." Blagger ducked his head. "Long time
back."

"Let me see the rest while we talk. And you can ask the
more impertinent questions as well." Burrows tapped
Blagger's wrist with one long finger. "How is he?"

"Passed on five years back. Fair down."

"Authorities?"

"Yeah. Holed him and he lost it."

"Pity."

"May I?" Blagger reached out cautiously. Burrows offered his other arm and loosened his tie. The tattoos were shaded between black and purple, depending on their age. The lightest ones were wisps of outlined stars and rings from his simplest thefts.

Blagger's own were still dark comparatively. Only the very first few were faded to purple. It was these simple black and purple tattoos that most of the sugars were aping. Most of them probably didn't even remember why anymore.

"Of course, my boy." Burrows smiled encouragingly. He was justifiably proud of his career.

The multi-colored spiral at the top of his shoulder,,, mentioned that he was seeing profits from not one, but five governments. Sister saint, he couldn't even tell. The Lady could read the signs though, so maybe Penny would be smart enough to get close-ups of the marks. He looked up, startled. "Five?"

"Five." Burrows looked pleased. "Doing my level best to make it six, I am."

"And the arrangements don't conflict?"

"Oh, they conflict a bit." Burrows took off his vest and Blagger mirrored the motion. Oh, this wasn't one of his seductions, but the technique would make the connection that much stronger. Without vests and ties and shirts, they were just two thieves from London learning as much as they could from each other. It was so much easier on the streets. No layers of cloth to hide the symbols. You could tell at a glance who was who and the Sugars none the wiser. The Authorities didn't care to learn.

"And they're lucrative?"

"You've been on this Estate too long, old son. There's money to be made for an enterprising young man. I might have an opening soon."

"Oh?"

"I've been given to understand that my man is being held. I don't know what he's done, but I won't bail him out."

Blagger leaned forward. "He forced a bird, then croaked her." He narrowed his eyes as the rage surged through him. "A married bird at that. In the business too, ain't she? Ain't right."

Burrows' eyes widened and he sat back. Genuine shock then. "Dear God. Are the Authorities on the way?" His voice dropped. "It's a fair cop then?"

"Video clear. Sure there's more, but that's enough for me."

"Blast. And Lady Long knows?"

"Yes."

"You've pigs then?"

"Plenty."

"Just pack his things and I'll dispose of them."

"Authorities are on the way for more'n that." Blagger kept his voice low. He moved his fingers in what would appear to be a random pattern on his arm to let the man know that they'd make it look as though his man had run off. It made no sense not to have him on their side for that at least. "What's hot this year?"

Burrows' eyes cleared a bit and his shoulders relaxed. He unbuttoned his shirt to show off a bit more and Blagger again mirrored the motion. He was the younger in the room and it wouldn't do to be seen as bragging. Although, something deep in his stomach yearned to show off just a bit. To have Burrows pat him on the head or be impressed at least a little bit. "Technology, as always. Harder to mock than take. And satellite positions. Heard London's decided some of its are getting long in the tooth and need a little polishing."

"Anything a boy like me might get his fingers into? Mocking, I mean?"

"Genuine's better'n mock. True."

"True 'nough. Always has been. You specializing this

year? Or running something special?"

"Season's going to be long. Time for me to find someplace warm and quiet."

Blagger frowned. "Last Season?"

The older man nodded. There had to be a good fifty years between them. He'd had one blast of a run. Blagger leaned forward to read the story on his upper arm. Parts of it were faded, but it was still clear enough. Three people conned into buying the same faked painting, which had been stolen so many years ago, that authentication was nearly impossible. Intriguingly enough there was also a story about ransoming away an Estate near the Islands. His free and clear and the victims not willing to talk about it.

Burrows frowned suddenly, fingers reaching to touch the start of the story that ran across Blagger's collar-bone. "Oh, poor duck. Merton? I wouldn't wish him on my enemies."

Blagger shrugged. "Needed what he offered, didn't I?"

"Like a hole in the bloody head, you did. Did you drop him?"

Blagger was still for a moment. "Saw it, right enough. Weren't my finger though."

"Down hard though, yeah? Couldn't happen to a meaner son-of-a-bitch."

"Took care enough." Blagger remembered the sound of the cleaver hitting Merton's joints. He shook off the remnants of fear the memory invoked. Taking the motion as an invitation, he settled on the table, legs crossed like he would to work on a console. Burrows fingers were gentle and warm. He smirked at the younger man and tilted his head to the side to let him read the story that ran down his throat. "Merciful Mother of sand. He didn't really?"

"He did. Lost too."

"Ain't surprised. Stupid bet to make."

They explored each other's black and white stories. Burrows was from level 215 of London and lost his parents early. His first teacher was Birdy. Blagger was from

228 and his first teacher was Merton. Beyond that, there were heists and cons and a few love stories woven into the patterns. Burrows' finger ran along the line that whispered across Blagger's left shoulder blade. "You did? Who talked you into that?"

"Who talked you into stealing the Helion on the Estate you're stuck on?"

"Landon of Merrick, why?"

"Because London's headed right at us." Burrows laid his palm flat in the center between Blagger's shoulders. The door chimed. "Lock door, Code 558!" Blagger snapped out.

"Fuck," he heard as Velvet's fist hit the door. "Open the door."

"No. Back down, luv."

Burrows chuckled. "Boyfriend?"

Blagger grinned as the older man circled around to sit in front of him again. "Is he cute?"

"Very. Fine voice when he sings out too."

"What do you mean London's headed for us? London's got redundancies and hovers."

"They've been broadcasting Maydays for the past," he consulted his pad. "For the past 20 hours." He grimaced. "When they hit us, it'll open up floors 300 to 1000. No question. And it'll knock us out of the sky."

Burrows' skin took on an unhealthy ashen color. He shook his head to deny that. "They shouldn't be moving in this storm. No one should."

"We might be able to save the children. Who wrecked the ships?"

The thief stilled. "My ship wasn't the only one targeted? I'd thought you'd done it to tip my hand."

Blagger shook his head. "Went up on an inspection and found every single ship in the guest area broken."

"There are others on the Estate then. Not me or my man, no matter what else he's done. Ain't stupid enough to shoot out our only way off, am I? No. Didn't come from me."

"Who do you like for it?"

"London? Get rid of some of the spice, blame it on someone else. Nobs shake sad heads and write us off?"

"And scrambles the entire Season of Autumns."

Burrows blanched at that too. "Not my plan, sure 'nough."

"Can't steal from corpses. But you know who the other agents are. Ain't no way a man like you comes here without strong intel." Blagger leaned forward. "Who else is dead in the water?"

"Belgrade."

"That was eight parties back." The young man shook his head. "Idiot should've spread the word."

"Might have lost their comm chip in a poker game."

"And lost their first born in a go fish game?" Blagger's eyes widened. His fingers twitched. "I have to set up a game." He heard laughter in his radio and identified it as Gov's.

Burrows snorted. "You can print up your own cards and that idiot won't notice. Tell you true, son." He rubbed at his temples. "Circuit's in my room for here."

"And London?" It was a pure guess, but Blagger's gut was sure.

He grimaced. "You'll find it."

It wasn't London's stabilizers that had gone out then, it was their Helion. He considered. It might be the Helion and the stabalizers if they wanted the city to crash. "Your ship then? Love to get it back where it belongs."

"And be seen as the hero?"

Blagger snorted. "No. Hopefully make sure my mates don't breath atmo."

"A worthy goal. Nothing's flying." The older man paced. "There's a prototype radar that can see through smog."

"Beyond the heat watchers? Those things screw up with the electrical."

"Wells was bragging about developing it. It might be on the Estate itself." Burrows bent his head and rested his hands on the back of the chair. "Don't know if it'll work with something the size of the Estate, but he'll turn it over to the Longs."

"For a fee? Or if I scratch him?"

"Make him piss and he'll do it. You flying blind?"

"Wheelman died this, no yesterday morning." Blagger rubbed at his eyes.

"Swear down?" Burrows frowned. "My idiot do that?"

"No eyes."

He stepped closer to the table. He ran a finger over the starburst scar that ravaged three of the stories on Blagger's right shoulder. "Stripped down from the skies."

"Burn bright." Blagger's voice felt tight. He didn't want to watch it, but he knew that he was the witness for this. He'd done this, backed his first crush and oldest role model into a corner. Burrow's lips twitched up into one last smile.

"I do wish I'd had the chance to teach you. You could have stolen the stars when I was done with you." Burrows dressed slowly. He handed Blagger his shirt, so that he didn't have to move. Mother, he was tired. Neatly dressed, both of them looking like proper Sugars, Burrows took his chair. He unclipped his watch. "Millipede built this one," he said. He opened the back to show off the works. All hand cut gears. He's got the tiniest saw I've ever seen." Blagger didn't stop him from palming the pill that fell out. "And he reconditions old watches. He'd be a good one to go to for repairs. Might even convince him to come play under the floors with you, if you smile sweetly and offer him some metal."

He closed the back once more. Then, he reached across the space and clipped it to Blagger's vest and tucked it into his pocket. He yawned and covered his mouth. He winked. Then, he went rigid for a long moment.

Blagger watched until his shoulder's loosened and the

spark in his blue eyes disappeared. He swallowed hard. The Authorities would have put him into a dark little hole and blamed him for everything. It was better this way. He wouldn't waste away. "May the little sisters carry you to heaven," he murmured. He didn't know what Burrows believed in, but whatever lay beyond had to be better than a five by five Nob-hole.

# CHAPTER 17

There was pounding on the door, but Blagger didn't unlock it. He put his face in his hands. Gov or Marsden could over-ride the lock code. Or they could get Spinner to authorize it. He didn't cry. Tears had been kicked out of him years ago, but he wondered, just for a minute what it would have been like to steal The Stars from the London lords. The door slid open a few minutes later. Spinner's hands settled on his shoulders. "The Helion's in place. The directions are programmed and the radio is broadcasting. Metro found the London Helion and six other Helions in the ship," she whispered into the back of his neck.

Nurse took Burrows vitals, but everyone knew it was just a formality. She looked up from her crouch to glare at Blagger. "You could have stopped him."

"I have no idea what you're talking about, Nurse." Blagger lifted his head to meet her eyes evenly. "His heart stopped." It was the same diagnosis that anyone committing suicide or quietly murdered on the Long received. There was no need to borrow trouble.

Gov lifted one wrist. He stared at the tiny parade of cats with the uninitiated frown of a Nob that wanted information, but couldn't read the evidence in front of his face. "What does it say?"

"Dream on, Gov." Blagger snorted. Gov wasn't a thief and never would be, even if he might have been a murderer. He was a military man through and through, no matter how much he seemed to have adjusted to the estate. "You want to know that, you get me drunk."

"That'll cost too much. Poker game?"

"War?"

"Dice?" Gov raised a brow. It was the best deal to make with someone who didn't know slight-of-hand. Blagger might actually give him a fair game.

"Dice." Blagger nodded. "But later. We need to talk to Mr. Wells. See if his radar is actually functional."

Gov perked up at that. He cracked his knuckles. "I'll have someone ask Mr. Wells to join us then."

"That would be me, I suppose," the Lady's voice said. She sounded cheerful at the prospect. "It's the least he could do for pinching me earlier."

"He still has hands?" Gov asked. Marsden joined them a moment later. He leaned against the table. His elbow brushed Blagger's. It was about as emotional as he'd let himself get.

"Tell me we have him?"

"He's dead because he didn't want to be holed for stealing the London Helion Circuit. Incredible that he managed it. I'd have to hack into his pads to see if he has notes on how it happened. His man, Weston, is the one who killed Sun-Yi. I don't think he's behind the ships though. He seemed genuine enough. And there's no way he'd lock himself into the site." Blagger leaned his head back to rest on Spinner's shoulder. They'd done more than their share on this one. There was just the two matters left, Branch's death and the damage to the guest ships.

"We'll go change and help up on the docks, then, I guess," Spinner said. He heard something in her voice that he followed.

"Good idea." He brushed his fingers along Marsden's

arm as he unfolded himself from the table. He rubbed at his knee. "I really shouldn't do that. Knee doesn't like it anymore."

"Getting old, Blagger." Marsden gave him a half-smile. "Give Mel a hug from me, would you?"

"Of course." Blagger nodded to Gov with his brows raised. Gov waved him off with a nod. Spinner wrapped her arms around his arm. She waited until they were in the hall to tap his radio. "Blagger signing off."

"Heard," Penny replied.

He tucked it away. Spinner did the same with hers without announcing it. They slipped down the back halls to the Crew transporter. Finally, they were in their quarters and changing out of the fancy clothes and back into the sturdy over-alls and equipment that made up their day-to-day lives. Blagger held the heavy gold watch in his hand for a long moment before he stored it away.

"Why did he do it?"

"Which part? The heist or the kill?"

"Kill himself. I would have thought that the legend would be appealing?"

"Five by five cell with a single light and no contact with the outside world unless there was serious money brought to bear and he never married."

"What will happen to his accounts then?" She frowned. "Or do thieves not bother with things like that."

"I'll hack them and transfer them to a few dozen people." Blagger scrubbed at his hair with both hands. "And enrich the Lady a bit. This place could do with some upgrades after all. And I'll have to tell the story some day."

She tightened the belt of her pouch. "Tell me that you don't have a pill that will kill you on your person right now."

"Oh, sweetheart, I won't lie to you." He left it at that.

She went hunter still and stared at him. "Don't you ever dare," she ordered. "I will get you out."

"I won't use it unless I'm cornered too deep and you're

not around."

"Promise me. Promise me on whatever will make you keep it."

"I never make promises."

"Promise me."

"I promise that I will not use it if there is any chance that you can get me free."

"Good enough."

He looked at her for a moment, but her eyes were darting around the room. He didn't know if she were looking for cameras, now that they knew about the ones on the Crust layer or if she just didn't want to meet his gaze.

He let her get away with it for the moment. He didn't think he wanted to know. "Let's go lock down the wheelhouse a bit more. You can double-check my headings and chat with your opposite number on the London."

"That might be a good idea." He put on his radio. "Marsden, sing out channel 55." He changed his radio to his personal channel.

"Marsden here."

"Have you told London that we've found their circuit? Do the Nobs know?"

"Let me step for a minute." Marsden found a quiet space somewhere. Probably throwing someone out of the security lock-up room. "I haven't talked to anyone on London yet. You have an idea of who's in the know? I don't want to start a panic. And I don't know who in the Authorities to reach out to. Not for this. Someone causing trouble, or a fraud, no problem. New papers for a child. Or to make new identities, who knows. To fence their circuit back to them, not so much."

"I want a bolt of whatever you're drinking."

"You can't afford my Stim."

"Are your fingers shaking cuz you should think about slowing down on that."

"I've got two murderers, a thief and a saboteur in my Estate. I am not going to calm down until they're all gone."

"Well, I don't know how we can really throw that many people off the dock and not have anyone notice that we're raining bodies."

Spinner sent him a startled look, then quickly switched her radio to his frequency. He winked at her.

"It's business as usual for a Season party, you mean? Yeah, I hear you. We haven't had anyone die here in a very long time. Well, not that we bothered to call someone in for. Still, who should I call?"

"Call and ask for Carmel London. She's the last navigator I talked to. We can see if her name's on the mayday warning or not. They still broadcasting their the same message?"

"Our new tether and the mayday? Yes. I heard your princess put out the word to the other Estates that we were moving in the fog. I can't tell you if they're coming back right now. I'm not linked up to the feeds. Tag Penny. So, Carmel London. And tell her flatly that I've found her circuit and would like to arrange a finder's fee? Or is there some arcane rule of engagement?"

"She won't have the authority to offer money, but she can probably take something back to her boss or the owners. But," he paused, not sure how to explain it.

"I knew there was a but coming. Is this something to do with politics that I don't want to know about?"

"I'm fairly sure that London or Lancaster paid for the circuit to go walking. Shadowboxer was working for London, Lancaster, Milan, Turin, and Ellis."

"Holy shit."

Blagger winced. "And sadly that doesn't even narrow down the suspects. Could be he snagged it for the glory and the ransom and got stymied by the smog, same as us. London shouldn't have started drifting if someone hadn't gotten to their stabilizers."

"What I'm hearing is that someone not only grabbed

the steering, they damaged the tethers, and debased the stabilizers?"

"Someone knocked it out of hover. We didn't even notice the Helion being pulled. It didn't bother our hover at all. It's not connected to the stabilizers."

"And you don't know if this is enemy action or a call to action?"

"Do I think one of the Londonium would be willing to sacrifice people to score political points in a war they haven't officially declared? Yes."

Marsden covered his radio, but Blagger heard the string of profanity. Spinner's eyes widened. "I don't know half of those words," she mouthed at him. "Was that English?"

He shook his hand side to side to indicate that it was a mixture. He held up his fingers and counted down as the man's steam started to fade. By the time he'd reached five, Marsden was back. "Contact Carmel and do some hypothetical probing for me. Get me a name and I'll do the final contacts and contracts. Hopefully, we won't have to involve the Lady."

"That would be unfortunate." The Longs had to remain neutral or they wouldn't stay in business. That didn't mean there wasn't a lingering loyalty to the London that had spawned the Lord and Lady. She didn't involve herself in outside business too often these days, but he wouldn't bet against her in a political game. "We need to save that for when we've really got troubles."

Marsden snorted. "True. I'm going back to the main channel. And remind Spinner that if she's got a business arrangement with one of the socialators she either pays the percentage back to the estate or works it off."

Blagger choked. "Sister bless. If she's seeing Little Miss, I'm selling photos."

Spinner punched him in the arm. She couldn't say anything without letting Marsden know she was listening in. She changed over to the main channel. Marsden laughed. "Good, she's off the line. I want a full rundown on the political players for this game. I don't care what you have to break to get it either."

"Right, boss." He changed over to the regular channel. "Blagger's on."

"Spinner's on."

"Then you'll be getting up to the docks soon?" Mica asked. "Can you bring up a bag of randoms? We're needing parts."

"I'll gather some right now." Spinner jogged her head toward the door. "Blagger's double-checking the heading for me."

He jogged to the quick pole and locked his safety harness to it before taking a deep breath. The trip unnerved him still. He checked the messages and the last known positions of the Estates and ships around them. Spinner had them heading back and to the right. Ameris was right behind them. Last heading looked good. London was still heading straight toward them. And shit, the Baldwin was next to them. They had to be moving too.

"Long to Baldwin. Are you moving straight back to evade the London's drift while we change tethers?"

"Baldwin to Long. Negative, Long. We're moving straight up and should clear your top level in twenty minutes. Hey, Blagger, where's Branch?"

"Branch passed on."

"Hard luck. Give my love to his little girl."

"Will do, Elko. Long to London."

"Go ahead Long, this is London."

"We've fixed our issue and are moving to the assigned tether. We should clear your heading within an hour and a half."

Carmel London snorted. "Magic workers on your Crew, Blagger. Mine are telling me they can't do anything in the storm."

"Just good luck, luv. You chat the walk."

"Been awhile, but I can hack the chat."

"Found some green locks while looking for our own

lock. Reads like a special star. Need a squawk with a non-Nob about it."

"Huh. Interesting. Got a stand-up Nob to blow the chat, if you like. I'll ask him to come over special for a date night."

"Plan him for the response to the broken Crust here."

"Let me chat. I'll call you back."

"Thanks, luv. Got a circuit map you can send?"

"It'll be in your pad in a few. London out."

The Lady's voice lifted into the chatter. "Spinner, sing out, channel 2."

Blagger changed to channel 2 as he started a quick visual diagnostic of the repair work. He made some notes as he listened into the Lady's conversation. "Spinner here, ma'am."

"I understand that one of the confidential issues has been taken care of. There are still two more loose ends. What's the status?"

"One of the issues will be taken care of before the Nobs. The other matter, the other matter is more delicate. I'd prefer to handle it in-house after the Season passes on."

"I'll leave it to your discretion. Do tie up a pretty bow for the Authorities, would you dear?"

"Of course, ma'am."

"And, Blagger, I expect that there will be an increase in my account shortly?"

"Yes, ma'am," he answered. "I'm off." He switched back to the general chatter. He wasn't sure he wanted to know yet, or ever. Everyone had their own pasts and he wasn't keen to press Spinner on hers.

"London to Long."

"Long here."

"Chav Blackhurst. Seconded to the Long investigation. Stand-up. Swear down."

"Thanks, luv. You'll have to meet me for a drink some time."

Carmel chuckled. "My husband won't stand for it

unless he gets to come to." They'd never actually met and never would. She was one of his Shadows from when he'd been on London proper. She just didn't know it.

"That's okay. I'll send him off with some of my Crew. When we fetch him back he'll be more than glad to have a drink with us."

"Watch your thrusters. London out."

"Clear skies, London. You read that Marsden?"

"Got it. I'll get some time with him when he comes."

"You coming, boy-toy?" Spinner had a bag of parts over her shoulder and her hair looked ruffled from her quick trip down the pole.

"You didn't use your safety strap did you?"

She rolled her eyes. He followed her into the elevator and up to the docks. His shoulders slumped. "There better be Stim up there."

"Kitchens have been sending it proper," Mica answered. "You two up for doing some real work now?"

"Possibly. That'll depend on what you haven't been able to do."

Blagger pulled up the work list from his pad. "Mother of moth-eaten parts, what did this little bastard do to that speeder?"

"Still needs to have its hover fixed."

"I'll look at it. Spinner's got a bag of bits," he said as they made their way onto the docks. He poured two cups of Stim and handed one to Spinner. She bolted it down. He sipped his more slowly as he reviewed the work.

"Blagger," Mica shifted uneasily.

"What is it?"

Mica twisted her fingers together. "It's just that you need to sleep. I've had everyone else on the cots for at least two hours. You and Spinner haven't yet."

"Can't sleep with all this racket. We're opening the transporters again. We need to close off the docks though. Pull the doors and make it look like it's just a preparation for the smog."

"On it," Tread called out. It was a simple action of opening the shield that they put up whenever they were opening the outer doors. The two were kept completely separate for safety sake. It had been Blagger's first action when he'd become the head of the Crew. He'd seen too many mistakes on London's many docks to trust a link between them. The shield folded across, blocking out the view from the guest rooms and isolating the entrance. No guests were getting in to cause trouble.

"Go lie down. Both of you." Mica took the Stim out of their hands. "Now."

Spinner stared at her as though she were speaking a new language. "I'm going to work on the speeder. Blagger do you want to hand me tools or try doing real work?"

"Very funny, princess. Let me have a look at the Stang98. I wanted to rebuild one of those when I was a kid."

"Didn't we all." Mica sighed. "Please rest."

"When this is done. Not before." Blagger gave him a small smile. "Mel, honey, I've got a hug to deliver from Elko."

Mel melted into his arms and he wrapped them tightly around her. She sniffled a little bit onto this shoulder, but her own arms wrapped around his waist. "I heard about Burrows. He was the one you used to tell me stories about, wasn't he?" she murmured into his ear.

He nodded and her arms tightened. "Had to be." He kissed her forehead. "Back to work with you." That gained him a the majority of a smile, so he called it fair.

The Stang98 belonged to Roseburg. No one had touched it yet. The speeder that Spinner was working on belonged to Dritz. Between them, they'd be able to search the vehicles for further evidence. One of them might be their saboteur.

He peered into the open panel and grimaced. The perpetrator had simply grabbed a handful of wires and circuits and pulled straight out. There were torn connections and resistors were scattered on the floor. He picked them up and put them into the pocket of his pouch. There was a slight chance that he could reuse them. He found the door circuit and used his driver to slide the door open to find the schematics that should be in the front compartment.

He flipped through the files on the pad that held the schematics, registration, and other information. He noted Roseburg's last five stops. At least one of them wasn't a Season party. He didn't know what it was, but he shouldn't have been there if he were just following along with the moving party that made up the Season.

"Need a hand?" Tread asked.

"I think I've got it for now."

Tread nodded. He leaned against the ship. "So, you got to meet him finally?"

"Did everyone listen in to that?"

"You kept your radio on." Tread shrugged. "We're all sort of programmed to listen to your voice."

"Suppose so." Blagger shrugged.

Tread pulled off his radio and Blagger did the same. "I just wanted to say, I'm sorry. No one needs to watch their idols fall." He quirked a half-smile. He patted Blagger's knee. "If you need it, there's whiskey next to the Stim and no one would begrudge either of you the use of the cots for a few. We'll wake you up while you're still hungover, of course, but we'll let you sleep for a bit." He winked.

"Brat." Blagger smacked his shoulder. "Let me work on this a bit. I'll consider sleeping when we're down to only fifty ships to finish up."

"Everyone hear that? Only way to get the boss to sleep is to keep him going until he collapses or we get down to fifty ships to fix." Tread's voice echoed across the docks without any enhancement. "Or, I could just punch you," he said more quietly. "Used to do that to unreasonable blokes in the bars."

"Don't even try it. Spinner'll kick your ass." Blagger

turned his attention to the pad. "Thanks for the concern."

"You need to spend more time with us normal folks. Those pricks downstairs are affecting your brainwaves."

"I have a brain to affect at least." His attention was fully caught by the files that were hidden in the subdirectory. He cursed softly.

"Blagger, radio back on." Tread took the radio from his hand and put it into place. "Don't want to miss out on anything more tonight."

"The chatter from the docks is comfort enough, I think." He smiled absently in thanks. He slipped the files onto his own machine. "Metro, get your tight ass over here. I have something that needs recording."

"I don't know if I should ignore the comment or thank you," Metro drawled. "According to Velvet you're very discerning about these things."

"Velvet's ass is nice too. Here, I need a record of the things on this pad. You've got the damage here already?"

"I did a walk through." Metro recorded the file lists. "What am I looking at?"

"Possible treason if London didn't put these on here. Military files. Intelligence agent maybe. But still, this is on an unsecured datapad in an unlocked ship."

"Unlocked? Wasn't the lock the thing that was damaged?"

"No, that was the launch and the cabin pressure. We need to check through the luggage compartment. Then, I want you to go track Spinner's progress on her ship. And have you isolated Burrow's ship?"

"It's locked and closed with a security strip that only Gov can over-ride." Metro's eyes darted to Blagger's collar, where just a hint of his tattoos showed. He didn't ask the question that was obvious on his face. "And we can do that to this ship and leave it damaged until the Authorities get here."

"Let's finish looking it over first. Simple enough to fix. They weren't at all concerned with making it impossible.

They just wanted to make it hard enough to stop a mass evacuation."

"The dock cameras aren't showing anything unusual. The person responsible wore a flight suit and a cold weather hood."

"And took how long to disable all these ships without anyone noticing?"

"We were looking for a murderer. Not watching the security feeds." Metro frowned. "Unless the murder itself was a distraction?"

Blagger shrugged. "I'm not sure if it's even connected anymore. The thefts, yes. But someone's messed up London too."

Metro's chin lifted. "London? What did they do to London?"

"Stole their Helion. Disabled their hover. Blasted the tethers"

Metro paled. "Does that mean what I think it means?"

"Not germane to this discussion. I need to make sure we've got records for the Authorities."

"Good for you. You said 'Authorities.'"

"Gov really should beat you more often."

"He's not into that. He's got that pretty little woman in the Kitchens."

"The red-head with the little pink bows she wears right behind her ears? She's a sweetheart." Blagger smiled softly. "I keep hoping that they'll finally get married. They've been engaged for longer than some people's marriages last."

"I don't know. Maybe she's not the marrying kind."

"Enough gossip," Spinner said across the radio. "Metro, come do some recording in the luggage area. Let Blagger get some actual work done."

"Bite your tongue, woman," Blagger chided. "Me. Work?" That being said, he did wade back into the schematics and reworked the wiring. He hummed lightly to himself. It was something sweet and sentimental he'd heard too long ago to identify anymore.

He lost himself in the wires and felt his shoulders loosening. This was something he could do without feeling in over his head. His pad chimed to tell him that it had finished translating the documents. He fished it out of his pocket and started to read. The blood ran from his face. "Gov, sing out."

# CHAPTER 18

"Gov, here." His voice was tired. "What's wrong?"

"Why would anything be wrong? You might want to talk to Mr. Roseburg about his ship."

"Is there any way that this day can get any longer?"

"Technically it's tomorrow for both of us."

"Don't help. Send me what you've got and I'll get someone to ask Mr. Roseburg to join us."

"Might want to intervene before he gets to his room and gets rid of the flight suit and winter hood."

"Burgess and Ilona, sing out."

"Burgess here."

"Ilona here."

"Get up to 1153 and ask Mr. Roseburg to join us in the security office for a few questions regarding his ship. Do not let him into the sanitizer or near the garbage shoots. Kitchens, sing out."

"Bismuth, here. How can we help, Gov?"

"Who's on garbage duty? We need to keep an eye for a flight suit and winter hood."

"Kerit, here. I've got the Environmental team. We're looking right now. We'll call when we find it and not touch it too much."

"As though it'll help?"

"I didn't say it," Kerit said.

Blagger sent the files from both the ship and Roseburg's room. Mother save them all from well-meaning patriots. He was going to start a war, just to make London look like a victim. Maybe if they were lucky he'd kill himself too. Then, they'd only have to make Weston's death look like a suicide and they'd be able to turn all three of the bodies over to the Authorities with apologies. They were a simple Estate. They didn't have the ability to keep political prisoners after all. He rubbed his forehead. He put the pad away. He already knew more than he wanted to about politics.

"Blagger, these documents?"

"Are from his personal pad and from the ship."

"And what program did you use to get through the encryption."

Blagger was silent for a long moment.

"Blagger, don't you dare go off radio or so help me, I will have Bastet drag you down here by your ear."

"I'll send it to Wheels," he said quietly. He sent off the program and deleted all traces of it from his own machine.

"Wheels here. Blagger? You'll need to run me through the authorization codes."

"You're a big boy, you can hack it, can't you?"

"Please?"

"Mother of Mercy. Mother of Sweetness. Mother of Stars. Mother of Love. Mother of Death. Mother of Moons. Sister of Anger. Sister of Bitterness. Sister of Plants. Sister of Hate. Sister of Life."

"Got it." Wheels was quiet. "Is that a litany or something?"

"Something like that." Blagger had been raised with a faith in the Mother and Sister. The Father and Brother didn't like to be bothered with thieves like him. The Mother was the only one with the compassion to understand that sometimes there was no other way to survive. He dragged his mind away from the quiet alcoves of the London lower floors and back to the hustle of the Estate. He finished fixing the ship. "Metro, Security tape this one."

He moved onto the next ship, then the next. Mica's voice broke into his thoughts. "Blagger, I need you here."

He crossed the docks and looked down at the small creature curled up in the ship's console. He chuckled. He picked up the little fluff-ball of a cat. She grumbled at him as he carefully returned her to the cage that was in the back of the ship. He fixed the door-latch that had given way. "The scary cat is gone now, dear." He ruffled Mica's hair. Mica swiped at him.

"And it won't get out?"

"No. I promise."

"You get to fix this one. I'm going over there now." Mica moved with stiff-legged dignity across the dock's metal floor. Her workbooks thudding softly as she did. Mel's lips stretched into a smile.

"Care to give me a hand?" Blagger asked her.

She joined him at the damaged panel. They worked quietly. She pulled off her radio and Blagger did the same. "Have you found out who killed Daddy?" she asked bluntly.

"Will you accept that I'm not sure, luv? Spinner might know for sure. But you'd have to talk to her. I've been much more focused on the missing circuit." He handed her the heat-iron and watched as she fixed the next part of the board. She was quiet for a long moment.

"Did you forget him?"

Blagger's heart ached. "Never, sweetheart. He was a good man and he loved you. And if I had my way, we wouldn't be up here fixing things that should never have been broken, we'd be in the Commons toasting and remembering him until the day was out. Then, we'd collapse, drunk on whiskey, tears, and laughter right where we were. And when we woke up, we'd offer him one last toast over the a mug of Stim and some painkillers."

Mel sniffled. Then, she threw herself into his arms and he held on tight as she started to cry. And as soon as this was done and his people had a good eight hours rest. Four at the least. They'd start on the wake and toast Branch and remember him and tell his stories. Unless, mother have mercy on them all, there was another emergency.

He rocked her gently, but didn't offer any of the useless platitudes that he'd been offered when his father had died. He'd been only eight, but he knew they meant nothing. No, remembering Branch and speaking his name and history would mean something. Branch had no faith. He had no clue what Mel thought about those sorts of things.

"Got you wet again. Sorry." She blew her nose on a rag. She scrubbed at her cheeks with the back of her wrist.

"It'll dry. Any time you need to cry on me, I'm here. Will you be willing to go over to London for a bit? Seems their crew is short handed. I'll send Tread as a guide."

Mel nodded. She held his eyes for a long moment. He didn't know if she could read the truth in them. He needed her away for safety. "I think it would be good to get out of here for a little while," she said quietly. He nodded. He put his radio back on.

"Gods damn it. Blagger, sing out!"

"Blagger here. What's wrong, Wheels?"

"Have you read these?"

"Some of them. Enough."

"Then, you know that the Lord needs to read these dispatches?"

"Yes, he probably does."

"You have some time to come down and talk to me about this?"

"I have an outstanding appointment. But then, surely." He switched his radio to Spinner's channel. "Little Miss?"

"There you are!" the socialator said. "Come see me so that I can get out of this damned dress and go to bed."

"No need to stand on ceremony for me. I'll be up in a

few minutes." He switched back to the main line. He waved at Tread. Tread left his twin working and joined him. "Take over here for me?" He flicked his eyes at Mel. "I need to fix something in one of the Sugar rooms."

"Christ. What else today? Really?"

"Don't jinx us that way." Mel punched him in the shoulder. She'd be fine.

"Blagger's off." He didn't put his radio into his pocket. Not just yet. He made his way to Little Miss' room quickly, looking down at his pad, as though he was getting ready to take care of an emergency. The Sugars politely didn't notice him in the halls. If he'd shown up dressed this way in the ballroom, they would have spun themselves into a tizzy. The gall of a Crust that was obviously Pit Crew showing up to spoil the effect of an entertainment would be fodder for the gossip for half the season. A Pit Crew member hurrying to fix something in a room was different. That was politely ignored. No one wanted to spend the night with a light that didn't work or a malfunctioning link up to the Estate systems.

He knocked in pattern Little Miss' door and she opened it quickly to usher him inside. She smirked at him. "This is like a fantasy holo come to life. Want to check out my... console?"

He laughed. "Hello, beautiful. Need help with that dress?" He tucked his radio into his pocket, to the laughter of Spinner and Mel. Let them think he was just making arrangements for the night. Or reacquainting himself with an old lover. It would be easier that way.

"You'll scandalize the woman that thinks she's my chaperone. So, you and that lovely little piece down in the ballroom?"

He shook his head. "Not her thing."

Little Miss blinked. "I've never met someone who didn't care for it at all. Truly?"

"Maybe a kiss to the cheek or forehead. A hug here or there. And she'll curl up on me to sleep." He shrugged.

"What do you have for me?"

"Oh, come in here and sit down." She waved at the rug. "As long as these are self-cleaning rugs. Otherwise, you get to stand in the sanitizer and talk to me from there."

"I'll sit in your closet and critique your wardrobe."

She laughed again. "I have missed you, boy-toy." She settled on the chair by the window. "You got my list?"

He settled on the rug in front of her, propping himself up with his hands behind him.

"I did."

"And did it help?"

"It did. I won't tell anyone where it came from." That was normally understood, but he didn't want there to be any mistakes between them.

"I'll just deny it if you do. This other matter is a bit more delicate." She crossed her ankles and leaned back in the chair in a way she would never do with a patron. She tapped his foot with hers rhythmically as she considered how to state whatever it was. "You know that I would never put myself in the way of a businessman and his acquisition target."

"Of course not. It's simply not healthy."

"Exactly. Would you like something to drink? I've got that green label you liked."

"That would be lovely."

She moved the small box from behind her chair and poured two cups of green label. It shone like citrine. He turned it in his hands and watched the light play through the crystal glasses. "Do you miss it?" She sipped her drink.

"On occasion. Not enough to ever go back to it though. I've aged out."

"As long as you're happy, I suppose." She sighed. "Now, as I was saying, I normally wouldn't bring this to the attention of a businessman, however, I have a lingering fondness for Violet. And now that I know you're here, I couldn't possibly stay quiet."

He looked up at her. "I understand. I would never ask

you to do anything that would compromise your companions." He gave her his most innocent smile. She laughed and her face lit up.

"Oh, my dearest, I would take you to bed, but I'm just bloody tired. Let's get to the point then. Drink your green label and listen to me preach."

He leaned back on his elbow and pulled up one leg. The position was familiar and he felt a pang of regret for the bridges he'd burned as he left London. He could be lounging in the courtyard of a Londinium and playing court to a lovely older lady and not worrying about oil under his nails or smog dirt digging into his skin.

Little Miss took a long moment to organize her thoughts. "I heard from Bruno Bertalucci of Milan that Herod Kingston of Turin had designs on the Long businesses in Turin and Petra."

"Turin and Petra?" Blagger sat straight up. "Oh."

"Yes. Oh. And Dear. And I believe you'd say 'Mother of mercy preserve me.'"

"Something like that. Was there any more detail to that?"

"I heard from Constance of Stockholm that she was in a business arrangement with Bruno and Herod both to work on the Long business threat in Stockholm." She paused. "And there seems to be a consortium of businessmen from Longress, that are looking to move into the Lancaster territories that Long is holding."

"Organized attack on the Long businesses only? Nothing in relation to their satellite attentions from London?"

"No, Long has maintained that they are nominally neutral in all political maneuvering on that level and so far as I can tell, everyone believes that. You will be careful, won't you? You won't go poking your nose into dangerous things?"

"I can't help myself." He batted his lashes at her. "I promise only that I will pass the information on quietly.

And I will give you this piece of news to spread. Shadowboxer has slipped between the veils, by his own hand. His estate will be scattered like stars and salt within the week."

Little Miss put a hand to her mouth. "Said true?"

"Sworn and blooded."

"Damn it." She sniffled. She dabbed at her tears with the back of her hand. "I'll spread the news. Will he need avenging?"

"He chose his path. He chose to fly free rather than be caged."

She grimaced. "I'll tell the tale. I will miss him."

"I wish I'd met him younger than I am today."

"You saw him on his way?"

"I did."

"And Security didn't stop him?"

"They didn't know enough to guess. But there won't be an inquiry of those here." His face hardened. "He was hired to start a war, though he didn't know it. Let it be told to Lancaster and London that their secrets are only secrets so long as they don't involve innocents in their actions."

"Is that a threat to Lancaster and London from Long?"

"No. It's a threat from Whispers and Shadows. From Stars and Stones."

She straightened up, eyes wide. "You're going to involve, oh my. I thought you cut ties."

"For this, even the mistress won't be on me to stay quiet. Worth your currency, London's Helion circuit was stolen. London's hover capabilities were sabotaged and they were set on a course they couldn't stop or correct in the middle of the smog-storm."

"I'll tell the tale. Helion circuit of a City. That's impressive." She rolled the cut crystal glass along her neck. It was a move she'd practiced often enough that it no longer looked studied. "Who managed that?"

"Shadowboxer."

"I'll spread the tale." She nodded. He finished up his

drink. "Now, your reputation is such that I should keep you another hour for that alone, but I have a feeling that you need to get back to something or else you'd be sleeping."

"Every ship on the docks was damaged. The Crew has more than half of them fixed now. I won't sleep until we're down to fifty."

"So nothing to worry about?"

"No, it's all just enough damage to take some time to fix, not to permanently ground any of the vehicles." He handed her his glass and stood. He bent down to kiss her cheek and she turned enough to catch his lips on hers. He laughed into the kiss. "Take care of yourself, beautiful. And you know how to reach me now."

"Wait a moment. I'll give you a direct contact. No more of this playing on your girlfriend's radio."

He blinked. "Spinner will just find out. Give me an address you won't mind her using as well."

Little Miss shook her head with a soft smile. The glasses clinked onto the side table. She gestured for his pad. She added in her contact information. "There, much better." She touched his hand with the gentlest of fingers. "And I'll be leaving with the Season. That doesn't mean I don't want to see you."

"We'll make arrangements when the next Season comes or you need a place to Winter. I think the mistress would enjoy that."

She looked thoughtful. "I think that would be an excellent suggestion. I'll speak with her. I don't feel like heading back to Washington."

"You're out of Washington now? Did something happen in London?"

"I found myself not enjoying the company of the men there. Washington has many more companionable people."

"And powerful people as well."

"As you say." She smiled.

"Have you considered establishing your own small Estate?"

"Oh! I forgot to tell you about that. I've an Estate. The Burlington. It's near Washington. You and yours are welcome."

"Thank you, luv. I'll keep that in mind, worst come or I get tired of working for a living."

She laughed. "Oh, I'll put you to work, just not the kind you'd mind."

"Now, I might just have to look you up." He gave her a wink and left the room and made his way back to the docks. He put his radio on. "Blagger's on."

Tread chuckled. "Now, that's the man we know and love. Is she pretty?"

"Ask Spinner." He opened the door with his code and locked it behind himself.

"So what's the word, Spin?" Tread called across the docks. "Is she pretty?"

Spinner tapped her wrench against her lips. "Yes. As pretty as any of his men."

"Brat," he teased. "She's a lovely woman and I won't hear anything against her." He took up the next repairs. His mind spun over the information she'd imparted. He had so much to do and not enough time. If he worked late, he might be able to get Burrows' accounts properly dispersed before the Nobs showed. And he needed to brief the Lady. She's do some discrete checking on her own.

Marsden might need to be given a heads up that there were going to be odd pressures even when the Season moved on. Oh, and Spinner needed to know that Little Miss might be around for some time other than the Season. He was sure that they'd get along if they had time to know each other, but she got touchy about the oddest things. A general night of passion or even light dating like he tended toward with Estate members was one thing, an old acquaintance from London might be something all together more. He'd never had part of his past touch this deeply before.

"Give me the tools. Walk over to that cot and sleep for at least two hours, or I will get Nurse up here to drug you," Mica stated. He pulled the pliers out of his hands.

"I'm fine."

"We're down to fifty ships needing repair. You will sleep. The rest of us have. Spinner, come collect your man and make him sleep."

"And why aren't you forcing her to sleep?" Blagger lifted his brows.

Mica just smirked. Spinner pulled Blagger over to the cots. "Because I told her that I wasn't going to sleep on one of these blasted cots unless you were underneath me."

"I'm just a glorified pillow. Told true."

"Hush. I want to sleep." He laid down and she crawled on top of him and tucked her head into the space between his neck and head. He wrapped his arms around her waist. He closed his eyes just for a moment.

# CHAPTER 19

"Don't they look sweet?" Marsden said conversationally. "I mean, you'd think that they were puppies or something. Not even a hand misplaced."

Blagger slit his eyes open. Memory flooded back. Spinner simply lifted her hand in an obscene gesture. She snuggled into him and he tightened his grip automatically. She smelled like oil and sandalwood and burnt wiring. He ruffled her hair and it stayed in the crumpled curls from the product that still lingered there. Marsden laughed at them.

"Get up, kids. Or I'll post the pictures all over the system." Gov's voice made Spinner's eyes shoot open. She looked around the docks, then rubbed her eyes.

"I thought someone was supposed to get us up after two hours," she accused Tread. Tread looked up from his pad.

"Me? I don't think so. You two needed to sleep. We're laying in the alcohol and food for the wake. I was given the task of looking after you. I had the last nap yesterday." He saluted them with a mug of Stim.

"Storm's still surrounding us. We haven't hit anything. Go, give Branch his wake. Unless there's something we need to debrief?" Marsden raised his brows. Spinner's nose twitched. She rubbed it on Blagger's shirt.

He shook his head. "Nothing that can't wait until tomorrow."

Spinner stretched without shifting her hips away from him. He steadied her form as she lifted her legs up and reached back to grab them. It was times like this that he thought about exactly how much of a waste it was that they'd never had a night of passion. From the shocked look on the older men's faces, he was sure they'd never seen her do it before. Or maybe it was the fact that she was using him instead of the floor that had them shocked. He smiled sweetly at them.

"Why thank you, Marsden, we will be heading down to the wake and unless the steering alarms go off, the Crew is going to be dark."

"I hear you," Marsden said. He raised a brow when Spinner rose up into a handstand over his head before dismounting from the cot. Blagger rolled out of the cot and then got up. He stretched more conventionally. He folded up the cot and moved it into the back halls. He studied the work lists.

All of the ships were repaired. There was nothing pressing in any of the guest quarters. The Sugars were likely all still sleeping off the drink and drugs from the overly long party the night before. "Is there anything that needs to be done before we go dark that hasn't been reported?"

Gov grimaced. He gestured to the two ships that were sealed. "We're putting a guard on these. You spoke to London?"

"About a concerned citizen? Yes, they're sending Chav Blackhurst. He's in the know about London's situation and their navigator says he's a quiet little mouse."

"Good enough. Lady'll need a formal report from both of you, but that can last a day."

"Any of you coming down or can we lock the doors?"

Marsden shook his head. "I can't. Not with the Season here."

Gov frowned. "I didn't know him well. I'll give my condolences to Mel privately."

"Good enough. We'll talk to you tomorrow then."

Spinner led the way. Tread and Blagger followed her chatting lightly about what sort of alcohol was in place, how much food the kitchens had sent down and whether or not they should put out extra pillows for the Crew to pass out on. Spinner looked over her shoulder. "I'll put money on the pillows and blankets already lining the commons. And I'll give good odds on the piles being neatened up so that no one trips over them when their eyes are crossed."

"Hey, we've got the good stuff, not the potato rot that they make on the farm level."

"Liar," Blagger said cheerfully. "That is the good stuff. Works quickly and only has a fifty-fifty chance of killing you."

"I don't even want to know what you used to drink." Tread shook his head. Born and raised on the Estate, he'd never even visited a City. "So tell me about this woman last night?"

"Someone I knew before I ended up here." Blagger shrugged. "We were just getting re-acquainted. She doesn't care that I'm not in the City. She's a socialator. That means she started out same as me. No real money or even a good name. She made herself smart. Learned what people want and need and now she's gotten herself an estate and a reputation as a brilliant self-made woman." He smiled. "I'm so happy for her."

"She's got an Estate?" Spinner lounged against the back wall of the transporter. "I didn't know that."

"She told me at the last minute. I don't think she even thinks about it much right now."

"Did she try to steal you away? Because I won't stand for that," Spinner stated. "Because then Tread and Mica would take over the Crew and I just got you broken in."

Mica snorted over the radio. Tread laughed outright. "I know to just let you do whatever the Hell you want. It's easy. But I will not share a room with you. We'll put you in with Mel."

"What's that? Did someone try to seduce Blagger away from us? Never going to happen," Mel said. Her words were starting to slur slightly already.

"Started without me, luv?" Blagger asked.

"Just a couple. This is pretty warm in my stomach."

"Eat something," he ordered. The transporter let them out into the commons. Blagger and Spinner escaped to their room to divest themselves of their tools. Spinner reached into her cleavage and pulled out the small diamond she'd lifted. She tucked it away with Blagger's pocket-watches with a smirk.

"I'll put that somewhere else in a little while."

He shook his head. "Whatever you like." The commons was loud from voices. "Crew is going dark," he announced.

"Heard. You're dark," Penny responded. The chatter from the radio cut off, leaving only the sounds of the wake that was already started. The piles of junk to reclaim and the small projects to be fixed were covered with thick welding blankets. It gave the room a softer edge. The mass of pillows in the center of the room was made up of pillows to sit on as well as pillows from the beds and extra blankets that they used when the winter season came upon them. Blagger settled onto a purple pillow after getting himself a cup of the deadly clear rot that the Farms made. It wasn't green label.

It burned on the way down his throat and made the muscles twitch. He didn't choke, but only because he'd had practice at it. Spinner settled behind him and he slid down so that he could rest against her chest. Her chest was very comforting. She settled a hand on his chest. The other held her own cup of rot. Banner was telling a story about

Branch and one of his many conquests.

Mel was laughing at the story, but her eyes were rimmed in red. She'd been crying again. No one would blame her for that and she wasn't vain enough to try to hide the evidence. She looked beautiful, if young, and he wanted to grab her and hide her away from the world. Some instinct in the back of his mind let him assess her against the scale he'd used for finding new apprentices for the socialators he worked with. She had the smooth skin and she soft coloring of her father. Her eyes were dark and generously lashed. She'd grown up sometime when he wasn't looking.

"I remember when Branch found out that Lila was pregnant," he said softly. He wasn't sure to whom he was talking, just that the story wanted to come out. "He smiled so much that he looked almost pained. He chattered to anyone who would listen about all the things he was going to teach his kid. And he told anyone who'd listen that he'd make Lila his wife if she wanted. Lila just rolled her eyes and smacked him across the arm with a spanner. They were the sweetest couple I knew. And when Mel was born, I couldn't imagine them being any happier. They loved her so much that they'd have done anything for her." He smiled at Mel. "And she's grown into everything Branch promised and more. Cheers, Mel."

She lifted her mug and took a deep drought of it. Blagger slipped his own drink. "I remember the day that Daddy taught me how to weld. He let me wear his protective goggles and they kept trying to slide off of my face. He must have taken a hundred pictures that day as I made those first clumsy joins. He was so proud of me that he hugged me and spun me around until I ended up vomiting right onto his shirt. He just laughed. He left me to get cleaned up and I remember fixing the glasses so they fit right by making my own strap. And when he came back he rushed me to Drake to show off everything I'd done." She lifted her glass. "To Daddy and Drake the two most hyper-active grown men I've ever known."

The room raised their glasses. The stories continued to swirl around the room. Blagger's ears perked up when he heard the quiet gossip of Branch seeing Adelaide—Gov's fiancée.

"She's taking it hard, but she can't let that robot of a lover know." Grimes sneered.

"Don't rag on Gov too hard," Corina said. She jerked a head in Blagger's direction. "Not where someone who has to do something about it can hear."

Grimes glanced at Blagger, then paled. "Oh, damn."

Blagger stared into the middle distance as though lost in thought. He didn't want to hear bad things about the heads. He was required to do something about it, that was true. But beyond that, they were friends and he hated losing friends.

He was going to lose Gov somehow though; to Nobs or a quick bullet.

Maybe he'd move to Burlington and run Little Miss' estate for her. Spinner would never forgive him for that. Spinner's fingers dug into his hair, flexing and releasing as though he were a cat lounging in her lap. He bent his head back to look up at her face. She was staring into her drink. She looked at him and raised her brows.

"You didn't know? They're very good to you." She gave him a smile. "Just because you can lie well, doesn't mean you need to. Yes, Adelaide cheated on Gov."

"I prefer to assume that she and Gov have an agreement in place."

"Ask him about that would you? Just not without witnesses. I don't want to bury you too."

"He won't kill me." Blagger smiled up at her. She tapped his nose with one long finger. He turned his attention back to the stories that swirled through the room. Branch had gone through more than his fair share of lovers in the years he'd been the wheelman. Spinner's fingers threaded through his hair again.

"Are you sure?"

"As long as I don't move in on his lover."

"So you see the danger?"

"Sweetheart, we share a room. I'd be blind not to see danger."

She pulled his hair. "That is not what I meant an you know it."

"Let's not talk about this anymore. Not today. Today is for Branch." He kept his voice soft.

"This is for Branch," she replied. Her voice dropped to a whisper that was for his ears only. "And I don't know how to get Nob-quality evidence, short of trying to get a confession."

"And a confession would be bad? Too many neat knots today?"

She rolled her eyes. "My brain wants to just take care of the issue, but the Nobs are on the way, I don't want to cross them."

"That is a salient point. And if you're suggesting what I think you're suggesting, then I understand the need for caution." He grimaced. Please let me have misunderstood her, mother. In his heart he knew he was right though. He'd be losing Gov sooner than he wanted.

"Tell me about the day you met Branch," Spinner ordered.

"I really don't remember it that clearly. I had a concussion from smacking into the hull on a tether-wire."

Mel wobbled as she walked over to join them. She flopped down next to Blagger and curled up with her head on his chest. "Tell me I'm pretty."

"You're a gorgeous girl, Mel. And anyone who doesn't see that should be dropped off the docks." Spinner told her. "And if one of these boys or girls told you differently, we can make sure they never again get lights when they try to switch them on."

Mel giggled drunkenly. She was only sixteen, but like all Crew members she'd been drinking since twelve. She'd likely be dead before twenty-five. At forty, Blagger was one of the oldest Crew members. "I thought I'd lose him to an accident," she murmured. "Like Momma. I never thought someone would hurt him."

"No one can predict what will happen." Blagger let his arm curl around her waist. "Are we too heavy?" he asked.

Spinner shook her head. She massaged the back of Mel's neck. "He makes a very good pillow doesn't he?"

Mel smiled into Blagger's shirt. "He does. Mind if I borrow him for awhile?"

"Feel free. I would never prevent someone from being comforted by him."

"Or more?" The young woman raised her brows in amused question.

Spinner shook her head. "That is between you and him. But last I heard, he wouldn't make love to a woman under the age of eighteen. Something like ethics."

"Bite your tongue," Mel said. "You better promise to teach me sex when I turn eighteen or I'll go snuggle someone else."

"You're on my Crew, dearest, darling, little girl. I don't date Crew."

"Because Spinner would smother them in their sleep," Tread told her as he came to refill everyone's glasses. "Time for another toast, kids."

----------

As the rest of the crew slipped into alcohol induced sleep, Spinner slipped away to the wheelhouse. She leaned against the wall. "Lady Long, sing out" she called on the private line.

"Lady here." Lady Long was in a quiet place.

"I didn't wake you did I?"

"Spinner, hush. I'm more interested in what you have to report."

"The Helion is back in place. Blagger's negotiated to get the London Helion back into their hands. He's going to send two of the Crew over to London to help with repairs.

Not sure how he's arranged that."

Lady Long chuckled. "Don't worry, I'm sure it will be no trouble. London will owe us. And the other matters?"

"Sun-Yi's mistress has given us the go-ahead to take care of things on our own. And Weston's sugar is dead, but he gave us clear indulgence before he died as well. Pretty little bow for the thefts as well. The thief confessed to Blagger on camera before he died. There's still larger matters of state, but I'm sure you'll want to hear those from him, not me."

"Yes. And the last matter?"

"Emergencies are solved. We'll need to wait until the Authorities are gone. Branch's death will stay Estate business."

"And once his daughter is safely away?"

"That's up to you, ma'am. Accidents happen every day."

The Lady was quiet for a long moment. "You wouldn't mind?"

Spinner snorted. "Don't worry, ma'am. I'll solve the situation. You and I will know the truth and when Mel is a little older I'll let her know that the situation was dealt with properly."

"Thank you, dear. Now, go snuggled down next to your Crew and get some rest."

"Goodnight, ma'am. Spinner off."

"Long off."

# CHAPTER 20

The buzzer of the weather system broke through the radios that were supposedly still blacked. Blagger groaned as pain zig-zagged through his head. He dragged himself out of the stack of bodies. Spinner opened one eye. He shook his head at her. He went to find his way into the weather readings. He yawned and squinted at the screen. The light was far too high in the commons.

His shoulders loosened. "Good news," he said quietly. That noise still set off little shocks of pain. "The smog's cleared. I'm going to open the storm windows."

"I hear you," Marsden said. "Go ahead when you're ready."

"Let me verify the systems are clear." He looked through the results. The air was as clean as it ever was. The storm blinds blinked a bright green when he pinged their status. "Setting blinds to open slowly on the below decks and main levels. What's the read on the guest quarters? Should I open up the shields or are their hangovers worse than mine?"

"Open them. They should be at brunch right now. If not, well, they likely have their head under a pillow anyway."

Blagger snorted. The blinds throughout the Estate folded back into the hidden recesses of the hull. Sunlight, bright and harsh after the days of artificial light spilled through the main rooms and washed through the Farms. The commons of the Pit didn't have windows. Blagger pulled on his tools and harness. "I'm going to check the wheelhouse," he murmured to Spinner. She nodded, but didn't get up. Mel was still asleep in her arms, looking more like a child than she had in years, even with an empty bottle of rot in her hands. He took the transporter out of deference to his head.

The sunlight was dazzling in the wheelhouse. He could see the traces of Branch's death on the floor still. He'd need to bring down some extra harsh chemicals to clean them away completely. He took a breath and started moving the Estate to its new tether. They were free-flying and he could feel the pull of the engines that weren't used to moving.

Generally, once tethered, an Estate didn't move unless their status had changed up significantly. The closer to the bottom of the city and closer to the actual Earth, the higher the status. His brows rose as he realized that their new tether was almost at the wheelhouse of London. He laughed to himself as he felt the tether connect. There was still play in their mooring, but it was better than free-flying.

The radar positioned all of the Estates around them near to where they should have been by his calculations. He cheered at that. Something had gone right. London was drifting toward them though. He ran through several calculations. Sweet mother, she'd be on top of them in just a few minutes. He set the Estate into a gentle reverse to give the City more room. They pulled at the outer edge of their tether.

He stared out through the wheelhouse window at the shadow that was creeping across the sky. Then, she was there. Barely missing them as it brushed by. He could almost count the welds on the hull that was across from them. It was painted in the cheerfully strange colors of her flag. The leading corner showed all of the colors. He couldn't help himself and waved at the ship as it passed. Let some child on the lower levels see it and laugh. "London to Long, nice to see you too."

Blagger laughed. It sparked little firecrackers of light behind his eyes, but that didn't matter. They were alive and London wasn't going to hit them. "Nice to hear your voice, London."

The City continued through the space in front of them before coming to a halt and drifting in the opposite direction held to her position by a loose tether to the Anchorage that held the Cities to the North Pole. He watched her. She was impressive, massive. He examined his heart. He didn't miss her at all. There were still people he missed, but he loved the Estate now. "Long, this is the London Authorities. Prepare for our landing."

"Long here. Docks are open. Green lights should be showing," Blagger answered. He hoped that his voice didn't betray the way his heart was beating. "Security will meet you."

"I hear you, Blagger." Gov sounded groggy. "Simone, sing out."

"Simone, hears."

"Meet the Authorities and conduct them to my office."

"Right, Gov."

"Kitchens, we're going to need rooms," Marsden took over the waves with orders. Blagger listened with half an ear for any orders that would require his presence. He stepped into the commons. He frowned. He didn't want to wake anyone just yet, but the Nobs would want to talk to most of them. If anyone bothered to report Branch's death to them. He was Crew after all and it wouldn't be suspicious for him to be declared dead without an investigation.

"Blagger, sing out."

"I'm here."

"I need you and Spinner up here. And don't dress up," Gov said.

"Right. Should I bring anyone else? Mica ran most of the repairs on the ships."

"We'll send for people as we need them."

Blagger crooked a finger at Spinner. She had extricated herself from Mel's embrace and was standing, looking completely at peace. "You don't even have a hangover do you?"

She grinned at him. "No. And I'll teach you the trick yet."

He offered his arm. She took it. He set the alarms to wake the room in two hours if he wasn't back. Mica could turn it off if he were up early enough. If not, the cursing would be amusing to listen to. He left a bottle of painkillers on the table after taking a dose for himself. Spinner laughed softly. She pinched his arm and tugged him into the transporter. He patted himself down and found that his pad was where it should be.

----------

There were four members of the London Authorities standing in the dock. The eldest was a grey-haired man with the sour look of a career security man. Next to him was an equally old and terrifyingly competent looking woman with a severe bun. She was wearing a flight-suit and had lubricant embedded under her nails. She gave Blagger and Spinner a narrow-eyed look. Two younger men in uniform stood slightly behind them.

Marsden waved Blagger and Spinner over to the group. "As I was saying, these two are the ones you'll want to talk to about the item we're not talking about. They've got the whole story." The career cop waved one of the young men forward. A familiar young man.

"Blagger Long, this is Chav Blackhurst," Gov said.

The Nob was tall, with bulky muscles under his uniform. The blue uniform's brass buttons shone in the light. He'd grown up very nicely indeed, Blagger thought.

He'd been a scrawny thing at seventeen.

They shook hands. Chav raised his brows. "You remind me of someone I used to know."

"I've been told I have that sort of face." Mother of Stars, he thought, of course he'd flirt. Kid never could keep it in his pants. It was one of the things Blagger liked about him. Still, discretion would be preferable.

Chav gave him a cheeky grin and a wink. "I was told that you might have found something of ours?"

"In the ship there. I'll just show you." They stepped away from the group .

Gov had claimed Spinner and was introducing her to the other officer. "I assume you'll want to take it back as quickly as possible."

"That's a guess, Whisper."

Blagger's shoulders tightened. "Blagger," he corrected softly. Chav shook his head with a fond smile.

"You never forget your first," he murmured.

That startled a laugh out of Blagger. "Well, in that case, should I call you Calvin?"

Chav winced. "No. You're right. Nice to meet you, Blagger." They exchanged sly smiles. Then, Blagger gestured at the sealed ship. It was a pretty little red ship with classic lines and a delicate star on the side.

"Shall I do it, or would you like the honors?"

"Please feel free."

Blagger slit the tape with his knife and opened the cargo door of the ship. Chav's eyes went large when he saw the bright green cube. "This is what everyone's been going mad over."

"I'd assume so. Let me get a loader."

"A moment. Who's ship is this?"

"It was Shadowboxer's. Going by Burrows while he was here." Blagger couldn't keep the sadness out of his voice. "His body's in storage downstairs."

Chav winced. "Oh, Hell. Help me get it loaded in the second ship and I'll get out of your hair. Winston can take the statements. Unless you'd rather I did it before I leave?"

"Depends on how desperately you want to get the City steering again."

"You really have been working Crew too long." Chav shook his head. "No one except Nav and a few of the uppers knows that we're not following protocol right now. There'd be panic."

"Then you've made arrangements to keep it quiet on the other end as well? I'd paint it, but I don't want to invalidate your contracts."

"I've got temporary paint in the ship. I can do it before it's off-loaded. Crew will make sure that it doesn't get damaged." The officer brushed a hand along the back of Blagger's and it made the hair on his arm stand up like an electrical shock. "Is there a quiet place we can retreat? I think I'd like to take your statement."

"Blagger going off-line. Mica, you've got the lead."

"Mica here."

"Penny hears." Blagger tucked his radio away. "Come on, there's a control room. We can talk there." He opened the control room. He jerked his head to the side and the Crust that was catching up on his reading scrambled out with a quick smile and a bob of his head. Cute kid, but still too young for any real responsibility. Blagger shut the door and closed the blinds. Chav settled on the floor, legs curled up. Blagger mirrored his position. "Mother, you look good. It's been years."

"I honestly never thought I'd see you again." Chav tugged on a lock of Blagger's hair. "You've never been the best correspondent."

"Letters and waves have never been my strong suit. I do much better face-to-face." Blagger let his lips curl up into a slow smile and he ducked his head so that he could look up through his lashes. It had worked much better when he'd had bangs that fell into his face. It made Chav grin though and that's what counted.

"So, tell me a story and I'll edit out what needs to be

edited out."

"Nothing wrong on our end of the tale. I don't know what you need to keep out of the reports on your side." Blagger ran him through the events of the very long day, excepting the death of Branch.

That would be handled on the Estate. It was up to Spinner and the Lady for that.

Chav took a recording and notes. He nodded encouragement and guided him through the standard questions. Letting Shadowboxer kill himself wouldn't count against him. No one expected him to act like a Nob after all.

Chav tied up the session. "I'll collect the evidence from downstairs." He took off his radio and tucked it away. He turned off his pad. "Now, tell me what you've been dancing around. Is there evidence of spying?"

"There is evidence that someone in either London or Lancaster or both hired the thief. And both sides would benefit from the damage done if London had hit us." Blagger shrugged with a frustrated snort. "I don't know how to read it."

"I'll look at it. There are a few good Nobs you know. Send me the copies you didn't delete when you gave the evidence to Security."

Blagger laughed. "Give me a secure place to put the files and I'll do that." He ran a quick knuckle down Chav's cheek. It had been awhile since he'd seen anyone from London who'd recognized him from before he'd worked his way up to the upper levels. "You're looking good, old son. You be careful and don't put your nose into dangerous holes."

"I have someone to pass the information on to, never you worry." Chav brushed a quick kiss to the back of Blagger's knuckles. "I would have thought you'd be married by now. Or the kept man on a lovely older woman's arm. The pretty slip out there?"

"Best friend I've ever had and brilliant besides. We

share a room, but not a bed."

Chav cocked his head to the side. "Only likes women? Makes sense for you, I suppose." He grinned. "Anything you've not told me?"

"Not that I can think of, but you'll get all your evidence from security. You won't be surprised if the bastard who killed Sun-Yi is a bit roughed up? And we didn't exactly take pains to keep him from hurting himself, I don't think."

Chav snorted. "I'm sure we won't see a thing. Even if he miraculously managed to find a way to kill himself. The Longs are a good family, after all. They'd never think such a thing possible."

"Stop smirking you. Let's go see if my pretty slip has kicked someone's tail yet."

Chav raised his brows. "Can she kick your ass then?"

"I am a lover, not a fighter." He paused. "I'm sending my welder and a chaperone back with you. They'll help sort out the mess I saw when we moved positions."

Chav blinked. "No one's supposed to know."

"My Shadows still whisper."

"Careful, I'll have to tell Mrs. Harrington your new address." The officer smirked.

"Shut it." They stepped back into the dock proper.

"Officer Blackhurst," Chav's boss said, "Run this evidence back to the city, then come pick us up. We'll finish up the interviews."

"Yes, sir."

Spinner slipped under Blagger's arm. She was vibrating with energy. "Do you mind if we get back to the crew, sir?" she asked Marsden sweetly.

The butler got a nod from the head Nob and sent them on their way. Down in the wheelhouse, Blagger looked at his partner. "Branch?"

She grimaced. "I've spoken with the lady. It will be dealt with within the Estate." She looked out the window at the impressive monster of the City that passed them.

"And I can't tell you anything more right now."

"Alright then."

"Little Miss had something to tell you?"

"I'll speak with the Lady about it."

She grimaced. Blagger's heart sank. They had secrets, just like always. "Did you want to leave with Blackhurst?" she asked.

"No, I'll never go back to London."

She nodded slowly.

"And if you run away, I expect you to take me with you," he said.

She laughed and hugged him. "I expect nothing less."

----------

The crew was neatly tucked into their bunks for a well-deserved rest when Spinner slipped out of the room she and Blagger shared. He was sleeping soundly, or at least faking it well enough to make it believable. Even the Sugars should be sleeping off the effects of being trapped in the Season party for the entire storm.

There was a camera over Gov's door, but Spinner redirected it with the access codes the lady had given her. With the camera effectively blind, she slipped into Gov's room. It was dark and quiet. His fiancée was on night shift in the kitchens today. Spinner let her eyes adjust to the dark room.

Gov was sleeping. She could hear him snoring and used the noise to cover her own movements. The white scarf over her head and lower face would tell him all he needed to know if he woke. He didn't shift, even as she carefully leaned over and dropped a distillation of herbs called Kali's Kiss into his ear.

The nurse would call it a heart attack.

Spinner waited until his breathing stopped. Then, she retraced her steps. She slipped into bed next to her partner. He rolled over and pulled her close. He didn't ask. She'd never tell.

They could tell Mel that Branch's murderer killed himself and she'd never know the difference. Branch was avenged and Spinner's honor was clean. She closed her eyes and slept.

THE END

# ABOUT THE AUTHOR

Kate Ressman has been writing for her entire life. It's true—she has proof of a second grade story where a cat inherits his human's money. A bit of a nomad in the past, she has settled down and currently lives in Northern Virginia. She has two businesses, a day job, and an imaginary cat.

*Sugar and Spice* is her second novel, and her first multi-part series. The next book in the series is expected early 2016.